metaxysm
RE HOLDING

Cliff Cave Books, LLC

This book is dedicated to all my family and friends who have supported me during the process of publishing my debut novel.

"Comparison is an act of violence against the self."
Iyanla Vanzant

contents

PROLOGUE

CIRCLE POINT. A POSH, well-known apartment complex for septuage-narian settlers that boasts a peaceful quiet. Although it's not off-limits to younger generations, the typical resident requires calm nights and low-drama days without the bustle of children screaming in the streets. Lights out no later than 9 p.m. is how it must be, dictated not by any association but by the residents themselves. This rule is also to be obeyed on weekends—a rule that successfully dissuades the younger crowds from even trying to lease a unit. Exceptions happen, however—very few exceptions.

A cluster of pines encircles the little community paradise, barricading the street from the rest of the city, with deep woods to the south whispering calm poetry in the breeze of the valley. Street lamps flicker to life, illuminating wrought iron swirls and manicured boxwoods—even the pavement glitters from chipped pieces of quartz and limestone embedded within. Only the buzz of electricity and rustling pines can be heard through the void. A visitor could mistake the community for a fairy tale.

Charles peers out his front door, blue robe parted ever so slightly, revealing a peek of ivory-striped silk pajama bottoms and no shirt. He looks left to right, making sure he's alone. Getting caught breaking the rules at this hour would most certainly subject him to ridicule at the next complex meeting, and no one wants to be ridiculed by the curmudgeons here. Alas, his bichon frise needs to pee. He's met with silence and emptiness.

He exhales sharply and tiptoes on handsomely quilted black slippers, the little white dog in the crook of his arm.

"Shhh, shhh, shhh, Bella," he warns the dog, delicately placing her on the ground. Obedient little thing, she does her business quickly and scurries back to Charles, tail wagging. "Good girl," he whispers, scooping her back in his arms. He takes a last look around for signs of a witness.

A small crash and tinkling sound break the silence. His heart leaps into his throat, and he turns on his heel to disappear behind the heavy soundproof door. A click and scraping sound secures him inside as the shadow of his gaze eclipses the peephole. The front room is now dark.

An in-ground sprinkler system springs to life, *click-clicking* a new song into the night. The moisture rains down over the perfect green grass and boxwoods, drizzling down the sidewalk. Swollen droplets arc under the lamplight, glistening as they drop fat and wet over the surface of squirming, pallid flesh. The smooth gray-green meat quivers and pulsates over the glittering pavement, creating a trail of thick, milky slime. When morning comes, no doubt the residents will not approve.

Each home's sprinkler system activates promptly, washing over the sidewalk and through viscous puddles forming on them. Great jellyfish blobs of the slime coagulate and rush to the sewer, revealing fresh and clean pavement once again, as if the mere threat of chastisement from the community reached out through each unit to activate the sprinklers.

A human pair of feet take tentative steps on the pavement, feeling each grain with a wriggle of the toe and an approving curl from the gray meat. The skin has a yellow hue, with a dark network of spider veins that can be seen just under the slightly translucent surface. The feet, with cracked and bleeding toenails, remain motionless on the spot, feeling the ground and learning more about their environment. More tentative steps, more learning.

The creature runs its tongue over layers of tiny teeth, relishing the taste of human life lingering on its palette. The sharp flavor of metal and warm protein lingers in its mouth—fresh, as if it had just eaten a raw steak made from a cut of this human. There is a distinct profile so strong that, with its inner eye, the creature can picture the contours of the human it tastes on its wretched tongue. In a moment of psychic connection, it is aware of the target's fears, pains, loves, motivations, and future movements. It knows where the target will be approximately fifteen hours from this moment, the exact amount of time the creature would require to travel there. The flavor has opened up the target's life to the creature—a knowing only reserved for them and God, perverted by the quivering mass of gray flesh. The sweet, lingering flavor of the human drives the beast forward like a slave beckoning the call of a primal scent trail.

The bare yellowish feet once again begin their walk among the squishy tendrils, making soft pats against the pavement. Sunken black eyes set deep within a manlike head survey the environment, observing every plant, every building, every object. It understands the terrain and learns it well. It must return to this spot. It must bring its human. It must return for its children.

The tendrils curl and coil, some wrapping and unwrapping around the creature's legs, while others help the legs with traveling. A few others trail behind it, undulating through the air like a cursed cape.

In the distance, the creature spies a copse of pines that leads to a more extensive thicket. It plans to use the cover of trees to travel unhindered by unknown threats. The yellow feet clatter toward the copse, making tiny patters over the surface. The feet levitate once the aid of two slick tendrils begin to roll by its side. The *tut-tut-tut* of night sprinklers fades, and the pallid flesh ducks under cover, away from the spotlight of streetlamps.

Once inside the cover of trees, the creature puts its yellow feet back down, sucking in fresh air through its mouth with a long extension of the human chest. Pressing its tongue against the roof of its mouth, it holds the scent inside, searching for the target's signal. After a few moments, the scent is captured, and the mass disappears farther into the thicket.

As it weaves through the trees, a blanket of slime coats the trunks, dripping slowly down the bark as foul sap. The creature moves slowly, observing its surroundings...learning. It hears noises in the distance.

***

"Just one last hit, Duane. Then I'll go clean." Jerry rolls up his tattered flannel sleeve to uncover a bruised, pockmarked arm. Using his teeth, he ties an old rotted rubber gasket around his bicep and flicks his inner arm.

"Whatever, man. Do what you want is what I say." Duane leans against a tree, the needle already deep into a vein. He smiles in relief, revealing a broken and rotting mouth tucked inside tufts of unkempt beard hair.

Jerry makes his move to prick his vein but stops, the needle hovering over his arm. "Do you hear that?" His ears flex to pick up the sounds of the forest.

"Nah, man. It's just the drugs. Don't sweat it. Just lie back," Duane thumps down onto the grass, making snow angels with his arms as his eyelids droop.

Jerry hesitates, lifting the needle away from his arm to focus his ears on the foreign sounds. *This can't just be in my head. I haven't even shot up yet*, he reasons. Looking around frantically, he hears more crackling of twigs and soft squelching noises. His eyes find what his ears are searching for when he catches a glimpse of a shadow not far from his and Duane's encampment. He nudges Duane, whose body flops against Jerry's hand.

"Duane...Duane! There's something there. Get up!" Jerry hisses through his teeth. Duane moans and rolls over, twirling blades of grass with an index finger.

Then Jerry sees it—not quite human, not fully alien, but a hybrid bubble of flesh and bone. It squirms through the forest, approaching the pair. The closer it comes, the more Jerry can see it has a very human head almost merging with a torso held high. It slides toward the pair.

"What...the *hell*?" Jerry's needle slips from his grip and hits the grass. His mouth is agape while his eyes labor over the horrible sight.

The creature looks down at him with black eyes and a hypnotic blankness as if blind to Jerry's presence. It glides along, cracking twigs and shuffling over the long grass while locking blank eyes with Jerry. Now he knows it's watching him—Jerry's bottom lip trembles as he slinks his shoulders back to make himself smaller. As the creature stares at him, the coiling tentacles sway behind it. It ambles on human feet, taking in the sight of Jerry and the rolled figure beside him in the grass. Jerry swallows a thick lump down his throat, feeling the burning gaze and terrified of the beast's motive.

The creature looks away, continuing past him. Jerry exhales sharply, his head dizzy from the fear trapped in his chest. It wades farther away from the pair through grass and mud. The pale gray-and-yellow flesh folds away into the shadow of the thicket.

Jerry fishes through the grass for the dropped needle and studies the barrel. He sees the liquid still inside, reassuring him that he didn't accidentally dose himself. He nudges Duane again, this time making him roll onto his back.

"Did you see that?" Jerry swallows hard again, his dry tongue running over cracked lips. "What the hell was that?"

"Yeah, dude. I see it, too. Pretty cool," Duane lies to Jerry and rolls over once again.

"I'm pretty sure that was a naked man, D!"

"You're high."

"No, I swear! It was a naked man! He was carrying a squid or somethin'."

"Now I know you're high."

Jerry cranes his neck to peer into the folds of darkness where the creature disappeared. The hybrid man is gone. He lies back down, glaring empty into the starless night, feeling his heart thrum in his ears and hearing the tiny voice in his head calling out to give up drugs.

***

The brute creeps through the woods on tender yellow toes, having found only two other humans that weren't the target. The rest of the forest is quiet and undisturbed, with only the sounds of singing insects and the scuttling of tiny beings that scatter at his presence. The beings are familiar—little hairy things with eyes that glow in the dark. Occasionally, he uses his tendrils to stand higher to gain a better view of the path forward. The furry critters dive through leaves and tall grass. Others perch in the trees, staring down at him from their towers.

Much time passes using the slow method of human foot-walking, yet the creature once again registers the sweet signal of the target from the air. Renewed excitement brews through his insides, rushing in a flow of warmth that spreads through his entire form. The sun peeking through the canopy of trees has been slowly searing his flesh during the long journey to this place, causing fluid-filled sacs to swell on his yellow skin. He prefers the coolness of the night and the cover it provided during the journey. Now, the daylight hurts his eyes and makes him slow. The trek hasn't been easy, with fresh raw pus leaking from foot skin as blisters pop and shred. The periodic mud wells are welcome pit stops to press his feet into, and he packs them with cool orange and brown earth. Travel time eventually dries and cracks his earth shoes, starting the process all over again until the next mud well. His inner voice screams at the pain, but he must carry on. The target awaits.

At last, he arrives at the end of his journey, the woods opening to a clearing. His feet drip with fresh earth shoes as he taps the protected toes onto a solid surface, not unlike the one he came from at the beginning of his journey. He breaks into a broad grin, seeing the structure from his dreams before him: a sleek black form tucked deep among the swath of old, giant trees. The structure stands proud and polished in the middle of the clearing.

A thin slime trail drips from the corner of the creature's wild grin. The human flavor that has been driving him forward intensifies in this spot. His inner voice recognizes the sights and continues to scream in protest, but the creature ignores the struggle of will. His blistered mouth cracks open to take in the aroma. He shakes his head back and forth while sucking in the surrounding air—the little hardened scales lining his neck rattle, filling the air with a snake song.

Dark eyes scan the black structure before him: north, south, east, west. He slithers closer to it, where the scent trail lingers stronger still. He opens his mouth again, more ooze dripping faster from the corners, making wet slaps on the earth below.

Deep inside, the voice grows smaller and smaller, but it knows this structure. It is a faint memory that tickles at the creature's frontal lobe, a grappling sensation between the lust for what the structure contains and the instinct telling him he might be insane. The scent pulls him against his weakened will.

The tentacles carry him directly in front of the structure, which reflects a malignant picture staring back at him on the polished surface. The heat-raised boils rise and fall, the largest of which is propped directly under his chin. It sinks and swells, making him appear like one of the forest creatures that leaps and likes the mud, too. He bobs his sickly head up and down, searching for an opening or weakness to exploit. Rising high on four thick, wet tentacles, he continues to admire his reflection on the surface. Slowly, he rears back. With great strength and the force of a wrecking ball, he launches himself through the side of the structure, scattering black shards in all directions and landing with a squishy thump in the middle of a large room. *At last, there is my human. At last, I will take what I want.*

Chapter 1

THURSDAY

THE WEEK HAS FLOWN by, with Thursday cropping up so quickly that Abby resigns to the fact that she, yet again, has no invention to show.

She constantly laments the descent into her lab, knowing the sun is shining out here and not in there. Soto Labs stands before her, casting its long shadow across her and the parking lot as the sun rises behind it. *Couldn't have been a rainy day, could you?* She sighs, feeling the guilt of trading the bright atmosphere for a basement and nothing to show for her time that week. The sun forms an angelic halo over the peak of the looming building.

Taking in her last breaths of fresh summer air, Abby drags her feet through loose gravel and cracks in the parking lot's pavement. With a building as pristine as Soto, the tragic state of the parking lot leaves one to wonder where the lab's priorities lie. The entry door swings open automatically to allow her entry into the foyer. She takes one last deep breath to savor the outside before forcing herself inside.

The locked inner door of the foyer stands ahead. Abby swipes her badge at the rectangular black reader positioned alongside it in one lazy motion. The beep, click, and whir of the locking mechanism signal the building's approval of her credentials, allowing her entry into the central atrium. Abby is immediately hit with the ritual smell of cleaning agents above the stark dryness of ultra-purified air. The pure air dries out her sinuses and has been known to occasionally gift her with a nosebleed.

An assortment of assistants and office personnel wander around, gathering their bearings for the shift ahead, each person making distinct sounds across the floor with their shoes. A handsome blond man with wide light blue eyes struts straight toward Abby with a grin and swagger.

"Good morning, Abby!" the man blurts out. She could have sworn he was lying in wait for his moment to talk to her. Abby thinks he smells pretty nice today, perhaps like lime and musk. He is always clean-cut and dressed well. Not a wrinkle can be seen on his pristine light green button-up and black pants.

"'Mornin', Tyler." Her throat clicks in the dry air, and attempts to clear it nonchalantly.

The well-dressed, fragrant senior accountant swoops beside her to walk the short distance from the entrance to her destination. He already has his coffee in hand, so fresh she can still see the steam rising from his dark green and lemon-yellow Traquatori University mug.

"How are things 'down under'?" He smirks, nicknaming her station in the basement.

Abby isn't humored by this and sighs audibly. "Oh, same stuff, different day," she says, eyeballing the steaming coffee, wondering if Ben had made any yet. "I hope to make it down there to get some of that." She nods and points at Tyler's mug.

"Ah, of course. Don't let me get in the way of your coffee. I'll catch you around, yeah?" He begins to back away. Abby nods and turns her back to continue her trek when she hears him shout after her.

"Oh, and before I forget, there's another happy hour tomorrow after work if you can make it. You have my number!" His last sentence is a distant cry as the gap between them grows. Abby's face splits into a fake smile while she pokes a thumbs-up. Turning, she rolls her eyes.

Bunch of immature alcoholics and posers, she thinks, considering the twenty-something crowd of random office-level acquaintances. *What could a thirty-three-year-old plain boring inventor possibly have in common with them?*

Despite Abby's regular no-shows to happy hours, Tyler never hesitates to invite her. In a way, she likes attention from another person, but coming from Tyler, she isn't as fond of the attention. She continues her journey through Soto toward a pair of double glass doors with another small black badge reader. She swipes her card again, is greeted by the same *beep-click-whir*, and enters.

In front of her, several of her former colleagues swish, wearing their white coats and scurrying to and fro. The floor biologists don't bat an eye at her presence. Fortunately, she doesn't have to cross the busy intersection—rather, she turns sharply left with the full intent of avoiding catching anyone's eye and encouraging small talk.

I'm not hooking up with him if that's what he thinks. Abby has heard rumors of happy hours and the bouts of debauchery that occur after the night at the bar ends. With no absolute proof, she still assumes Tyler has been a part of these rituals. She has no desire to partake and end up as a petri dish of random diseases.

She takes long strides toward the imposing black elevator that leads her farther into the depths of Soto. Just like the outside of the building, the elevator is looming, dark, and intimidating. It's eager to swallow her up and shuttle her to the underground depths where her elite job—and hopefully coffee—awaits. She steps into the pristine interior: another badge swipe and a press to button B6.

I mean, last time I went to one of those, some jackass said he would choke me out with his... Ding! The elevator chimes as the black doors close, and the last morsel of light converges into a sliver, then nothingness. The elevator then hums and pulls her downward.

Tyler really isn't that bad-looking, though. He's twenty-nine and younger, but he's already begun to make a name for himself in the accounting department. Abby can appreciate a little ambition in a man. He's slender and not terribly tall, but still a good three inches taller than her. She likes his dusty light hair and bright crystalline-colored eyes, but she has a hard time getting past his crooked nose. He must have broken it at some point, or maybe several points, as it's pretty cock-eyed.

The elevator thuds, knocking Tyler out of Abby's head and back to her surroundings. Before dumping off its payload, the elevator dings again—cheerful...mocking. Abby walks through a dimly lit corridor surrounded by alternately rotating rings that create a low, ominous hum while moving. Byron Todd, her quiet, brooding coworker, once told her these rings are meant to filter out miscellaneous radiation and other outside contaminants and what she and her crew bring on their person into the lab. Tony Donnola calls it "taking a steel shower," but Abby refuses to call it that. Ever since her first trip through the metal worm, she felt that whatever magic was being done to "cleanse" her would eventually steal her life force. That is, only after the dry, purified air above had its way with her. She swipes her badge one last time to get into the room at the end of the worm, and the door clicks open.

Abby steps into a wide circular landing that faces ten identical black doors evenly spaced around what looks like a large metal mosaic trapdoor. The walls are made of flat, cold steel, wrapping around the cylindrical room until it meets a clear glass spread, revealing the break room and the tenth black door directly to the left of the entrance. To the right of the entrance are doors 1 and 2, which are the restrooms, and doors 3 to 9, containing the labs and storage. Abby makes for the break room door.

"Look who's here," a gruff, bearded man in his late fifties announces as Abby slowly opens the door and slides inside as if trying to conceal her presence.

"Hey Byron," she says quietly while he works on hanging something on the wall, balancing on a small stepstool and leaning particularly close to said wall with some tool that doesn't appear to be a hammer.

Two other men sit at the communal table discussing weekend plans. They both look up at Abby. The dark-haired man on the right with his dapper long-sleeved button-up shirt smiles brightly at her, while the partially balding man on the left hunches and glares. His eyes turn into tiny slits.

"Anything good going on this weeke—" Abby starts.

"Not really," the partially balding man replies before the words completely leave Abby's mouth. He stands up and leaves the break room in a hurry. She watches him go with a narrowed gaze, then slides her flowery printed lunch bag into the fridge.

"Don't mind Tony," the dark smiling man says as she sits across from him. "He's extra mad today because his ex is trying to get him for more alimony."

She chuffs and moves toward the coffeemaker. One full pot of hot fresh coffee, still steaming, and another quarter-filled pot, looking cold and dead, sit there waiting for her choice. She feels around for her company mug in the cabinet and pours a nice black cup from the steaming carafe.

"Well, that's not the entire truth, Ben." Byron has eavesdropped without taking his eyes off the wall. "He's also a numbnuts."

Abby snorts and coughs while raising her fingers against her mouth like an abashed schoolgirl.

The underground crew is fully aware that Tony isn't fond of Abby. Ever since landing the inventor position, she couldn't figure out why. The only reasons she could muster are for one; she's a relatively younger hire; two, she's a woman; and three, the first two reasons, mixed in with the fact that she has one of the more prestigious roles at Soto Labs as an apprentice inventor. She knows Tony gossips about her to whoever will listen, telling them she seduced her way into the role. The rumors have hurt Abby, but she tries to let Tony's japes and continual sneers slide. She likes her job too much to let her pride get in the way. On occasion, she has wondered how she, of the entire qualified applicant pool, got hired into this role.

"Got anything new in the pipeline lately?" Ben asks, smiling with light hazel eyes and an infectious energy. He's always so upbeat.

Abby smiles back at him. "Nothing new yet, but I've been brainstorming some ideas that I'd like to try out either today or tomorrow. How about you?"

"Well, actually..." He looks around, eyeing his surroundings, "I've been working on a prototype I call the Truth Orb. I know it's not very creative, but it's a start."

"The Truth Orb?"

"Shh! Not so loud."

"Sounds mysterious," she whispers, taking a loud, tentative sip from her coffee. She swallows hard, underestimating its heat and further scorching her dry throat. "What does it do?" she croaks while fighting tears.

Ben shrugs and sits back in his chair with a mischievous grin. "Ah, well, it's not quite doing what I want it to do yet, but I'm working on it. Maybe I'll show it to you before lunch or something."

"Really? You'd show it to me?"

"Well, sure, but please keep it between us. We both know how important privacy is around here."

Abby is definitely aware. The tradition of keeping secrets started with Jon DeWitt before her time and most likely was due to idea theft. She's often wondered if Jon himself has stolen an idea or two.

"I also need to make sure it's not dangerous in any way before I show it to you," he says.

"Oh, now...you need to learn to take risks!" Abby says, putting fists on her hips while throwing back the bit of advice he had given her once himself. She nudges him on the shoulder. Ben gives her a slight smile and chuckles.

"That reminds me," Abby breaks in, taking a small tentative draw of the boiling coffee, "have you seen Jon's new gadget yet? He has been working on it pretty diligently this week, but I caught a glimpse of it yesterday."

"That crusty tool, I knew he had something! But Jon is Jon. You won't ever know it until something big comes from his lab. Between you and me, beyond his serious business etiquette, he really likes surprises. I dare you to sneak up on him sometime," he says, chuckling.

Abby titters, knowing that sneaking up on Jon is the worst idea. He's a severe man, senior inventor, and proprietor of Graviton, the beloved strongman of inventions. Graviton makes the company a steady fortune for its ability to lift objects up to two tons effortlessly. Jon has been part of the underground lab family longer than any other inventor currently employed. Neither Abby nor Ben know who Jon reports to, only that they report to him. Ben has told Abby that he suspects Jon reports directly to the man behind the curtain.

"I'll pass on the sneaking." Abby laughs. Ben laughs along, looking down and shaking his head. He stops and looks up at her through thick, raised, deep-brown eyebrows.

"You said you caught a glimpse of it, though?" he whispers, "What does it look like?"

"Yeah, I did." Abby matches his whispering tone. "Why are we whispering?" She sniggers. He looks at her with his brow still raised. Seeing him peer above her head, Abby turns to see Tony has returned, standing next to Byron and staring back at her. She turns her head quickly back to Ben.

"Just curious!" he says with uncanny cheer, abruptly sitting back and straightening his shoulders. His left arm twitches strangely, and she hears a faint pop of a knuckle or two. Ben clears his throat and looks back up at Tony. He rises from the table and slowly pushes the chair back into place, making awful scraping sounds across the pristine quartz floor. He reaches for the handle of his mug to pick it up and walks around the table. He stops to bend toward her ear with another whisper.

"Be careful what you say around certain people, Abby. I'll catch up with you at lunch...say around noon?"

She nods and lowers her mouth to her mug to hide her face as Ben turns on his heel to leave the break room.

That was odd...

The truth is, despite trying to impress Ben with her cunning and skills, Abby does not, in fact, have any new ideas to try right now. She only earned the title of apprentice inventor around six months prior. During her first five and a half years, she spent her time at Soto as a biology drone—one of the swishing voiceless numbers that scurries in the corridor by the elevator. To her, the work she undertook as a floor biologist was ordinary and dull, and she made no friends there. Ever since her first day, she was assigned to a particular test she ran and reran for every sample that others had crafted. She felt the test itself was very time-consuming and a waste of resources. The testing was vague, only giving answers akin to flipping a coin on a yes or no outcome. While cranking away on testing the samples, she'd occasionally eavesdrop on the chatter between senior biologists and catch a peek at some of the projects they were working on.

Their work is generally a tightly kept secret, like the work in the B6 underground. Any information she'd glean from her observations would be like finding the single-colored centerpieces of a million-piece jigsaw puzzle. Abby envied the senior biologists and was determined to become one. To make this happen, she kept her head down and chose to spend her free time innocently asking questions of the "right" people and making a great impression on them.

She spent hours researching the hierarchy of the department and days researching the various role responsibilities. Unlike Tony's assessment of her, the work Abby put into landing a role as an apprentice inventor wasn't earned by deceit but by grit and determination to learn more about the company. Her research often directed her into unlikely conversations with Tyler. He was the one to share the new opening with her. At the time, his account management revolved around materials and budgeting of the inventors, and he just so happened to have come across a newly created position of apprentice inventor.

During her six-month tenure underground, she's quickly learned not to let Tony's barbs connect. While he's been critical of her from the beginning, she doesn't allow it to dictate her mood or her tenacity in her role. However, she still feels a twinge of impostor syndrome and can't reconcile her merit for the position.

Ben proved to be an immediate ally for her. She dreads the days he takes for vacation unless Tony is also taking vacation time. Her tenure as a biologist was so unlike B6. The only friend she made, if you could call him that, was Tyler, who wasn't even in her department. Other than that, her world upstairs was boring but drama-free. Abby shakes off the memories and leaves the break room, mug in hand and wondering what Ben meant about being careful about what and what not to say around certain people.

creation

ABBY STROLLS TO LAB number seven. The executive team at Soto has designed the lab in such a way as to maximize privacy among inventors. Like a prisoner in a cell, each inventor has a solo area closed off by a locked black door and a single small window. Her lab may as well have a prison chuck hole.

The door directly across from the entrance, or room six, contains general equipment and tools. Each inventor has access to this badge reader. Following doors one and two (the restrooms), doors three through five are the lab spaces belonging to Ben, Tony, and Byron, respectively.

Door seven is Abby's, while door eight is an empty lab awaiting another new apprentice, and door nine is Jon's. Being somewhat close to his lab is how Abby was able to get a quick look at his gadget in progress. Her moment of fate came during a brief excursion to the break room, the precise moment Jon lifted his creation at eye level, which was conveniently in line with the little window in his door. She could see this invention was green this time and no bigger than a banana. He held it over his fingers as if custom holes were underneath the green banana. She may have lingered a little longer than she should have out of curiosity, but thankfully, Jon didn't spot her.

Each area is explicitly programmed for each inventor's badge. Abby couldn't enter Ben's lab, and he couldn't enter hers. There is, however, a master badge that a very secretive stock person carries that can access every lab. Abby doesn't know who this person is or when they work, but she has dubbed them the "night elf." The arrangement of the lab cluster offers each inventor a slice of solitude and privacy, and it has become commonplace for all of them not to ask questions about each other's work. If an invention goes into circulation, the inventor is given the appropriate attention, such as in the case of Jon. The fact that Ben is willing to share his Truth Orb with her is a sign of great trust.

Abby makes her way toward room seven and swipes her card for the fifth and final time after entering the front doors of Soto Labs. The door clicks and automatically swings open. She strides into the lab area, remembering Jon's green banana and its infinite possibilities, then hears the door close behind her, clicking to lock.

"Lights!" she shouts, to which the lab responds by lighting up in the incandescent glow of fluorescent bulbs. At the far end of the lab space is another office, where she begins to make her way.

Her lab is obsessively arranged, everything tightly in its place, not one thing missing or out of the ordinary. Abby's lab space starkly contrasts her office, which is a mess of paperwork, broken parts, and other miscellaneous failed prototypes. She enters the chaotic office and plops her bag onto the dirty, cluttered floor.

Ever since she started working in the underground, she's been trying to make a solid impression with the other inventors but comes short day after day. Most of her prototypes fail, with the ones succeeding having very little use outside of being odd party tricks. These inventions remain languishing in miscellaneous drawers in her office, not to be seen by her colleagues. Not knowing what to do with them, Abby relegates them to the pile of failures in hopes of figuring out how to dispose of instruments that possibly contain a myriad of toxic metals and liquids encased in unstable plastics. She figures one day, the casings will corrode and take her out, but the thought doesn't dissuade her from continuing to pile the failures in her office.

She wonders how Ben's lab is set up and if it compares at all to hers. Ben is always talking about great inventions, but Abby has yet to see any of them, as he generally keeps them closely guarded. Their conversation this morning has changed her feelings on that, and she now has something to look forward to after lunch, which she hopes will spark ideas of her own.

As Abby sits hard in her soft chair, the foam whistles and sighs at her. She taps her fingers in contemplation over a patch of uncluttered desk and looks up at the small, beaten silver holo monitor hoop resting in front of her keyboard. Her computer is old—cobbled together from other disemboweled computers to make one somewhat functional piece of crap. She "lovingly" refers to this as her Frankenputer. As she's an apprentice, it didn't entirely surprise her when they gifted her Frankenputer. She has first to learn how to crawl, and then she can run. And what better way to crawl? With a busted-up, unstable, and very manual instrument of garbage. She assumes the new apprentice they'll eventually hire will inherit Frankie.

"Frankie," she says, to which the grotesque monstrosity whirs and lights up.

"Go-o-od mor-ning, Ab-i-gail P-p-prin-ce," it stutters to her in a voice blended with robotic male and female tones as it begins its boot sequence.

"Good morning," she whispers with a sigh, bracing for the long boot time. She gets up and walks into the lab area while the computer tries to start.

Abby looks around the space, observing the rows of colorful, malleable metal panels hanging from pegs on the right wall. On the bench under the panels is a series of brown bottles, all the same height in a row against the back edge. Each bottle has a clean pipette attached to the side. The middle of the lab contains two island benches with several drawers and shelves. One bench includes several pieces of glassware ranging in size and shape. The other bench contains a variety of kits that have been given to her by chemists, which contain anything from basic acids and bases to more complex exploratory formulations that only work in specific situations. Abby sometimes questions using these formulations in her projects due to her numerous prototype failures.

She walks over to the metal panels and pulls a small matte-green piece off the wall. She pauses.

"No," she says, knowing she's being influenced by the memory of Jon's green banana.

I can't steal an idea, she reprimands herself. Returning to the metal panels, she spots a row of unfamiliar ones. She reaches up and pulls a shimmering blue piece off the wall. Walking back to the bench, she flips it back and forth to stare at it. Then, after grabbing a small hammer-like tool from one of the top drawers, she gently taps a corner to see how genuinely malleable this unusual piece is. It makes an ethereal *tink* sound and has a prolonged ring like a tuning fork. The more she taps the piece, the more overlapping rings echo through the lab. She isn't as familiar with working with this type of metal, but she likes the sound.

"S-s-s-yst-em wa-a-rning," Frankie calls out from the office. Abby puts down her angelic piece of blue metal and returns to the chaotic room. Once she's inside, the holo screen projecting from the silver hoop flickers with the warning in bold yellow letters flashing across the screen. She reaches over and hits the escape key to make it go away. Ever since Abby started in the underground with her junkyard computer, it has always done this. The warning is Frankie's signal that it has completed its boot cycle. Pressing it away is like ignoring the check engine light on a car. There might be something wrong with the computer, but it continues to run as Abby needs it to, so she's had no desire to have it checked out.

"T-t-ooo-da-y is Th-h-ur-s-s-d-ay," Frankie stutters in an eerie duotone once the warning message is ignored.

Abby briefly checks her email to see an empty inbox, like usual. She sighs, questioning her relevance in the underground, as usual.

Six months is a long time not to have a successful invention, she thinks, looking around the office, defeated. She considers her time at Soto Labs and the strange idea that ever since she's been there, she hasn't come across any other invention made by anyone at this point other than Graviton. These inventions are regarded as high-level mysteries ranging in usefulness and typically only utilized by those who matter.

Some inventions only serve as whimsical tools to explore chemical and biological connections to inorganic mechanisms. Others may enhance—or destroy—entire generations. To Abby's knowledge, no one has discovered a destructive machination...yet. For that matter, an enhancement invention can still fill the hole humanity doesn't know it has. Thinking about these things gets Abby excited to see what Ben has been working on. In the meantime, she walks back out of the lawless office to enter the brightly lit, well-organized lab space. She returns to the celestial-blue panel that makes music as she beats it with her small hammer.

The panel gives easily under the hammer blows, flattening more and more until a corner of the piece becomes so thin that it becomes slightly translucent. Abby holds the translucent corner up to her eye to look through it and is entranced by the reflections still within the metal.

This is pretty cool. Why have I never used this panel before? She puts the panel on the bench and scans the series of amber bottles. The bottles contain only about two ounces of material each, not nearly enough to craft a meaningful concoction from scratch. She turns to look at the shelf with the various kits gifted to her by the chemists. Moving over to it, she peruses all the neatly labeled, white paper boxes lined up like little soldiers. She reads the labels quietly to herself.

*Consternation... Alacrity... Bemusement... Furor...*Single-worded labels for each box of mystery.

*Metamorphosis... Miasma... Bliss... Ardor...*Many such boxes are stocked on the shelves, with at least five back-ups of each box—some with more.

Abby has used a couple of different ones here and there but has yet to be successful. As she scans the shelf further, she notices some new boxes that were delivered to her at some point recently by the night elf, which she is just now noticing. The boxes are ivory colored, with blue-lettered labels, as opposed to the white and black of their brethren.

She picks up one of the ivory boxes and reads the label: *Paroxysm.* There are seven such boxes with the same label, along with six other types. Abby runs her finger across the row of boxes placed just how she prefers by someone she doesn't know.

Genesis, Incongruity, Panacea, Percuro, Revivisco, Mors.

The ivory and blue color coding of the packages indicates they're from the floor biologists. Abby has heard of such packages during her time as a biologist, but this is the first time she's gotten boxes from them as an inventor. She's spent most of her time inventing using the white and black kits from the chemists. Seeing the ones from the biology floor renews her resolve, and it gets her excited to learn more about these confidential materials that she often heard tales of during her time on the floor but never had the opportunity to understand or use. Now that she has plenty of stock in both types, she's inspired to start creating revolutionary combinations. She grabs a pen from the holder on the bench along with a pad of purple sticky notes and starts scribbling down the names of the kits to take back to her desk and enter into her lab inventory. The inventory is where she can draw more information to create unique combinations of kits, dropper materials, panels, wires, and any other experimental object available to her.

"At-t-ten-tion-n-n req-q-quired," Frankie stutters boldly, only in the male voice. Abby swats the warning away and continues to patter on the keyboard.

"Hmm... Maybe Bliss plus Ardor plus Panacea," she whispers to herself. "Or maybe Metamorphosis, Consternation, and Genesis?" Her thoughts are a whirlwind of new information. "How about a double shot of Percuro, then Metamorphosis?" She continues to calculate several options before considering the consequences of each addition. Her train of thought is beckoning her to think first and ask questions later. After seeing all the kits from the biology floor, she wants to try anything.

She moves back to the bench where she was flattening the blue metal panel. After picking up the panel, she walks toward the ivory and blue kits and grabs the one labeled Paroxysm. Looking over at the black and white kits, she pulls out Metamorphosis. Slowly opening the Paroxysm kit, she sees a series of four vials inside and four syringes filled with different colored fluids. Each vial is labeled in small capital letters: endorphin, cortisol, catecholamine, and test. They appear as powdered cake in the bottom of each vial, which the syringes are meant to reconstitute. Each syringe is labeled according to each vial and contains about one milliliter of fluid.

She pops the plastic top of the vial marked test to see the target of the familiar rubber stopper beneath the aluminum seal. Grabbing the syringe labeled the same, she sees the fluid is translucent, like watered-down milk. She uncaps the needle and stabs the stopper. As she injects the fluid, the powder easily dissolves with the milky liquid, turning into a clear but sickly green in the process.

Very strange, she thinks, reveling in the unique reaction.

With one hand, she swirls the vial to completely dissolve the powder while fidgeting with the flap of the Metamorphosis kit with the other hand. This kit has the same layout but with two small ampules and no syringes. Each ampule is packed in liquid form with a breakaway glass tip. Abby estimates that each ampule contains around the same volume as the syringes from Paroxysm. The ampules have no names on them, only numbers one and two. In her experience, this is supposed to be the order of addition for each kit. However, there is no instruction inside, which hypothetically gives Abby the autonomy to make her own choice in the matter.

She remembers the way each kit operates: she must blend the contents of each kit in its entirety to achieve the effects each one is meant to provide. Therefore, she pulls a very small, ten-milliliter volume Erlenmeyer flask from one of the drawers in the other bench where most of the glassware resides, plunks an equally tiny Teflon-coated stir bar inside, and places it on a magnetic stir plate already present on the bench containing the kits. She carefully taps the number two ampule from the Metamorphosis kit on the counter to make sure no liquid is in the tip, then cracks it open and pours it into the flask with gentle stirring. In the past, she's always added the ampules in numerical order. This time, she decides to try something different, hoping for something that doesn't fail. Following suit with ampule number one, she gently taps and cracks it open, slowly pouring its contents with number two into the flask. Nothing extraordinary happens when she does this, and the blend mixes with no incident.

Hmm, no congealing, no smoking, no bubbling, and completely clear... I think this is okay.

Returning to Paroxysm, she pops the plastic tops of the remaining three vials and uses their respective syringes to reconstitute each powder. Again, nothing extraordinary happens other than a smoothly dissolving product. To extract each vial, she stabs the stoppers again with each syringe and draws out as much of the material as possible. In no particular order, she ejects the contents of each one with stirring in between, saving the green fluid for last. She watches the little stir bar spin around, creating a vortex in the fluid and mixing everything well. She is apprehensive about adding the liquid as she hasn't seen something like this before. Slowly, she untwists the luer lock that holds the needle onto the plastic syringe, revealing the blunt wide opening of the syringe. A small green bubble clings to the end of the plastic tip, threatening to drop onto the counter or her skin and create whatever havoc it holds. The more she looks at it, the more it appears like a poison, creating greater fear over ejecting it into her current benign mixture.

Abby pushes past her reluctance and squeezes the plunger tip down into the flask. The little stir bar continues to stir away, effortlessly blending the new addition and turning the rest of the concoction into a lighter shade of pale green.

No smoke, no fires, no explosions.

Abby lets out a fast puff of air from her lungs, having unknowingly been holding her breath. While the mixture blends, she returns to her metal plate and gets an idea. She begins to work again on the plate, hammering it thin and folding up layers with precision as if she were about to bake a flaky pastry square. The metal cries out in harmonious song in response to her meticulous hammer blows, filling the lab with a pleasant musical hum. She folds and folds the plate into innumerable layers without counting until she is left with a small square about the size of an ice cube. Each layer she has hammered thin to transparency, and the delicate cube almost seems to disappear when viewed from certain angles. She marvels at her handiwork, turning the cube back and forth, a smile creeping across her face.

Abby returns to her flask to see that nothing has changed, and her solution remains ordinary, with a pale green hue. She picks up the flask and pulls out a clear watch glass, which she places over a white piece of paper she removes from a drawer to view the color of the liquid over the black bench top. She pours half the contents onto the watch glass, which ends up being around a three-milliliter puddle. She picks up the cube and turns it in her fingers again, filled with excitement over this new object. The thin layers of the cube create the perfect set of channels to act as capillaries that she hopes will soak up the fluid mixture. She places the cube onto the glass, and just as she predicted, the little puddle shrinks into the cube. Leaving the cube on the glass, she pours the remaining mixture over the top of the cube and watches as it also disappears into the object. She gets more excited now, picking up the watch glass with the cube still perched atop and placing it delicately into her drying oven on the other side of the room. This particular oven operates at a low temperature but possesses a circulating fan inside to help coax the oven's contents into drying faster. She presses the button and hears the whir of the fan kick on. She waits just a minute until the oven stops, signaling that the process is complete and she can now remove her invention.

As she pulls out the object, she sees that it has transformed. It has become more beautiful, taking on the pale green hue of the liquid mixed with the light blue of the folded metal panel. It is now light turquoise and glossy, resembling the shallow end of an ocean tide. Again, Abby turns the object around in her fingers, where it still appears to vanish at certain angles. It hums with a faint rhythmical trill as she turns it—a pleasing outcome of one of the panel's musical attributes.

"Metaxysm," she says, naming her object proudly. The name is a simple combination of the two kits used to create it, giving it a mystery that matches the object's beauty.

She puts all her glassware into the lab sink to deal with later, meticulously cleans off the bench, and straightens all her things before taking her new invention into the office area.

To finalize the object's usefulness and activate its properties, Abby must connect it to Frankie. She returns to her machine, tapping different areas of the screen to open the activation program, creatively named "Animate." The program loads slowly, using a moving cartoon icon as a progress bar that starts as a seed, germinates, turns into a seedling, and then blooms into a tree. Frankie will cycle through this animation around twenty-four times before finally loading. Eventually, the interface becomes the tree part of the animation, with icon touchpoints running up the trunk. There is a physical pad plugged into the computer that's meant as a port for whatever invention needs to be connected to the program. The pad itself is a small, circular, soft, and flexible vinyl with three golden contact points that create the connection to the object. Inventions can be made in any size as long as the three contact points touch the gadget. When she sets Metaxysm on the activator, she perfectly matches two corners and one side with the contacts. Once she sets the proper parameters along the trunk of the Animate tree, she touches the "activate" button. Another progress bar begins to swell, which shows the tree as black-and-white and color slowly filling the trunk until it reaches the branches where new leaves bloom. The tree flickers back to black-and-white and starts to fill with color again. It will repeat this process until the invention's activation is complete—usually within one to two hours.

Abby checks the clock to see that her time in the lab has flown by. It's already 11:52 a.m., and Ben suggested they meet at noon, so she decides to stop for now and make her way toward the common lab to see if she can catch him and have him do a little show-and-tell with this so-called Truth Orb. Since Metaxysm's activation will take some time, she believes this is a good time to walk away.

Truth Orb... Silly name, not very creative, she audibly chuckles to herself.

Abby steps out of the office, making it about five feet from the lab door, when Frankie makes a loud beeping sound that echoes off the lab walls. She'd never heard this sudden beep before while using Animate. She peers back into the office only to see a normal computer screen, with the loading animation progressing. She hesitates with a twinge of fear for her new creation and watches the leaves of the animation tree bloom over and over with a ticking percentage counter climbing by one every several seconds or so. After watching for a while and seeing no further issues, she shrugs and continues toward the common lab.

Opening the door, she can already smell someone using the microwave. Byron comes out of his lab around the same time as Abby, and they make eye contact. He nods in acknowledgment and continues toward the break room. A moment later, Ben peeks out of his lab. He sees Abby and beckons her to come over. She looks around as if not wanting to be caught, then slips through his lab door. This is the first time she's been in Ben's lab since she's been there. Looking around, she can tell his lab doesn't appear to be any different than hers, other than the slightly cleaner office at the end of it. Rather than continue to gawk at his space and possibly offend him, she instead looks at him.

"Can I be in here?" Abby whispers tentatively.

Ben waves his hand like he's swatting a fly and directs her to a nearby bench. He is dressed similarly to Tyler today, with a light blue long-sleeved button-up and black pants. Unlike Tyler, there are deep wrinkles on the back of Ben's shirt. His thick, wavy hair is cut short, but Abby can see a little duck tail sticking out from the bottom of his hairline, touching his collar.

He places a red sphere about the size of a medium marble inside an evaporating dish already on the bench. As she gets closer, she notices a single button on the side that could easily be missed if one weren't looking for it. The button is the same color as the orb itself and rests flush with the rest of the object.

"Wow, is this the super-secret Truth Orb you were talking about?" she whispers semi-sarcastically with a smile as she hovers over the object.

Ben looks up and smiles without acknowledging either yes or no. "Here, just hold it for a second." He takes the little marble and pushes deeply on the dinky concealed button, holding it down momentarily. He beckons her to open her hand, to which she complies. He then presses the marble into her hand.

"Now close your hand over it," he commands, smiling in anticipation.

As Abby closes her fingers around the little sphere, it warms to her touch. Ben only looks at her, half smiling, without saying anything. Abby looks down at her hand and waits for something to happen. Her fingers are warm from the ball, like having an activated hand warmer clutched in her grip, but smaller. As her hand continues to warm up pleasantly, her forearm begins to follow suit and heat up as well. She looks back up at Ben, who still has the goofy half smile and an anticipative look in his eyes. As she continues to grip the ball, she notices that light emits through her fingers, illuminating the blood vessels and bones in her hand. The warmth and light spread, flushing her cheeks and causing her heart to beat faster.

"Are you trying to kill me?" she asks—semi-sarcastically again—with a slight color of fear.

"Just wait a second," Ben responds, slightly shaking his head to assuage her apprehension. He stares at her with wide brown eyes and an expectant curl in his smile.

As Abby waits nervously, she notices that her other hand, which has been perched on the lab bench the entire time, begins to glow as well. Yesterday evening, she reached into a cabinet at home and scraped her knuckle across one of the edges of the cabinet, shredding the center knuckle and leaving a painful scab that cracks every time she bends her middle finger. This scab begins to dissolve slowly, opening the wound again and allowing a little blood to trickle out, causing her eyes to widen in fear. As she looks up at Ben, he looks back at her and nods down to her hand. She looks back down to see the wound begin to close again, leaving the small drop of blood where the scab had liquefied. She closes her fist to wipe the blood from her knuckle onto her black pants and get a closer look at where the wound was. A little pink scar remains, which continues to disappear before her eyes as if it had never existed. Her skin tingles, and she feels the warmth of the healing, which makes her head swim and her heart pound. She lets out a small sigh reminiscent of someone who just got into a nice warm shower after spending an apocalyptic month in the cold getting filthy.

"Here, give it back quick," Ben says, extending his hand to retrieve the little sauna marble.

Abby reluctantly offers the marble back to him, breaking out of her trance. After she places it back in his hand, she begins to feel the room's coolness again, removing the color from her cheeks. She looks back at her knuckle to see a completely clear patch of skin.

"I take it this isn't the Truth Orb?" she states.

"No, this is way better. You saw what it did, right? Well, it's actually what I call the Knitting Sphere."

"The Knitting Sphere? That's not very creative..." She rubs her still-warm hands.

"Well, first of all, it started as a Truth Orb."

"Also, not very creative."

Abby looks at Ben and smiles, although internally she's screaming for the orb to be back in her hand.

"Your gadget can change the world." She cranes her neck to catch another glimpse of the sphere. She can't help but feel a twinge of jealousy.

"Well, sure, but when I was testing it, I could see it has its limitations."

"Like what?"

"For one, it only works on recent wounds. I don't know how recent, but I still have this scar on my knee from when I tore my ACL in high school about eighteen years ago, so not that 'recent'..."

"This wound on my hand." Abby holds up the hand that was healed, "I did this yesterday. Does that help some?"

"Maybe a little. I had something from earlier this morning that went away." Ben runs a finger over his chest but doesn't divulge what had been there.

"Okay, so we know then that it goes to at least the day before. I cut this knuckle in the evening, so it at least goes back fifteen hours. But why did my scab dissolve first and bleed?"

"Well..." Ben looks around. "I think that's how this little thing works. I think it actually turns back the time on your skin!"

"No way. It turns back time? Why did it look like I had a scar at the end then?"

"That wasn't a scar... it was the freshness of the wound before any blood came out of it."

"Does it just work on the skin? Anything internal?"

"As far as I can tell, I can't test out the rest unless someone tweaks their back, breaks a bone, or has some kind of organ failure. But in the case of the organ, most likely there isn't anything this orb could possibly do to fix that, but I really don't know yet."

"Ooh, maybe if someone gets stabbed, you can test it! I'm feeling a little stabby myself...with a certain balding creep..."

Ben chuckles. "Oh, stop that."

A moment of silence falls between the friends. After some time, Abby sucks in a short breath. "So far, this thing seems pretty meaningful to me. If I were you, I'd show this to Jon. Maybe you can get this in front of the higher-ups?" Her words are supportive but internally colored with jealousy.

Ben shrugs. "Maybe. I should probably do more tests on it before going in that direction. That way, I can tell whomever I go to exactly what it's capable of."

"It's your decision, but I think it would be good to start marketing it and making your claim—or getting a patent. Maybe show it to Byron first? He's pretty neutral and knows how to keep his mouth shut."

Ben nods and ponders her statement, biting his lower lip. "I'll think about it. Are you headed to lunch now? I was going that way myself..." He leaves the suggestion open-ended.

Abby looks toward the door and catches Tony's eyes, staring right back at her at that exact moment. "We probably should... Tony just walked by and saw me in here."

Ben's eyes widen for a moment, and then he shrugs. "Eh, who cares about that guy? He's a jerk."

They leave the lab and head to the break room, which now contains Byron, Tony, and Jon as well.

Jon is pacing near the back corner of the room, taking sips from a soda can and having a contentious conversation with someone on the phone. Abby watches him for a moment until he looks up at her. She immediately looks away as Jon frowns and heads out of the room. Turning her attention to the table, Abby sees Tony glaring at her. He half rolls his eyes and smirks, looking back toward his foul tuna salad sandwich and taking a large, messy bite.

She grabs her lunch bag from the fridge and remembers that she'd packed only a hodge-podge collection of convenience bars and some yogurt in her morning laziness. She sighs, unimpressed with her sad lunch.

Tony looks up at Byron and Ben, who just sat down, and engages their attention by rudely knocking on the table.

"Hey, I have something to show you guys. I've gotta new thingy I just finished today. I have to present it to the bigwigs tomorrow afternoon, so meet me in the common area in the morning, and I'll show ya." His invitation isn't meant for Abby, who chooses to lean against the counter and eat her bars rather than sit with the men.

"What category is it?" she asks.

Tony looks over at her in disgust. "Well, I'd say it's in the clinical category, but I'll leave that to the judges tomorrow." He spits out his answer and quickly turns away from her.

Abby smirks at Ben and takes another bite of her bar.

The din of Jon's conversation can be heard muffled through the glass of the break room.

"I mentioned that already," his barely audible voice comes through while attentive ears attempt to eavesdrop.

When Abby was a floor biologist, she used to read news articles on her phone during lunch. In the underground, her cell phone is useless against the steel worm and layers of lead that insulate the labs from outside forces. The same is true for everyone else's phone, except Jon, whose phone was specially given to him by some high-level suit at Soto Labs. Abby guesses it's most likely just an internal phone. Through the glass, Jon notices that everyone is trying to peer at him casually, so he walks back to his lab and closes the door. The crew continues the lunch hour in silence.

After lunch, Abby returns to her lab to check on Metaxysm. When an invention becomes fully activated, a nice feature of the Animate program is that it gives a list of elements characteristic of the object. Unfortunately, it doesn't tell the user exactly what it does, but the inventor, if they have the skill, should be able to extrapolate based on the information they're given. In Ben's case with the Knitting Sphere, he probably received characteristics such as "health," "healing," "time," or something to that effect. When testing out the object, this is how Ben determined, for the most part, what it does. Once Abby returns to Frankie, Animate shows her the list of potential characteristics of Metaxysm, her angelic singing turquoise cube.

*Excitement... Passion... Transmogrification... Rebirth...*and two successive circle symbols with a red *X* crossing through them, along with blank spaces where the elements should be.

Abby stops short at the two blank spaces with the corrupt reds *X*'s. She remembers hearing the beep sound before heading to lunch and wonders if Frankie accidentally corrupted two files in the process. She isn't familiar with how these symbols relate to the program and assumes they're under-formed elements that cannot be used. Disappointed, she sighs and considers crafting another Metaxysm.

Maybe on Monday... she thinks. Now that she knows how to build it, she can rebuild it and ask Ben if she can use his computer to activate it. She understands that by doing that, there is a minor breach of confidentiality, but she trusts Ben not to say anything since he trusts her in kind. For now, she has the partially complete Metaxysm and feels there's no harm in bringing it out for show-and-tell since it's most likely useless. The other four elements of excitement, passion, transmogrification, and rebirth sound promising enough that if Metaxysm does indeed work, it will be spectacular and possibly blow away Tony's piece of junk, which he's so arrogant about.

Abby sits at her office chair and absentmindedly runs a finger over Metaxysm, feeling the delicate edges she meticulously hammered thin. Her eyes are fixed on the cool turquoise gadget, and a musical hum begins to swell as her finger passes over the thin layers, putting her in a trance. The hum starts to crescendo, filling the office and her ears with ethereal music. She flicks her finger too fast against the edge and feels the sharp sting of multiple paper cuts.

"Ah!" She pulls back her finger and immediately puts it in her mouth. Looking down, she sees a small drop of blood clinging between two layers, which becomes absorbed into Metaxysm. Her eyes widen, and a slight cold sweat breaks out on her forehead.

I hope that was nothing.

Pulling her finger out of her mouth, she sees three identical slices across the tip, which begin to well up with blood again. With a sigh, she decides to call it a day of physical work and will finish out the rest of her shift working out ideas on paper. First, she debates heading to Ben's lab to see if she can borrow the Knitting Sphere again.

If Metaxysm absorbed my blood, I wonder if that changed it somehow. Or, maybe I could add blood to a future gadget. I'll have to try that.

Chapter 3

Betrayal

Thursday was forgettable for Tyler. It's Friday that's going to be the day and his anticipation for happy hour swells. He hopes Abby will be willing to show up this time, as he's in a particularly good mood. Perhaps being in the long days of summer has his spirits high and makes him feel lucky. He dared feel charitable as well and thought to stop by Duke's for a baker's dozen.

Carefully sliding from the leather driver's seat of his sleek red sports coupe, he balances the box of doughnuts in one hand with the handle of his backpack in the other. Rather than strap on the bag, he carries it by the top handle with a badge wedged between his fingers. He moves through the front two doors to make his way to the accounting office towards the back of the atrium. The motion lights respond to his presence by flicking on. Not a sound can be heard other than the low hum of the HVAC system and the buzz of a few monitors that some other careless accountants left on overnight. He carefully places the box of doughnuts on the small circular table in the center of the break room and makes his way toward his office, twirling his badge around an index finger and whistling.

Taking in a deep breath and relishing the early hours before his counterparts begin to arrive, he closes his eyes and thinks of ways to attempt to lure Abby to happy hour. He could entice her to meet him for lunch and work his charm that way. Or he could snoop through her company account and see if there's a bribe there. His slight obsession with Abby only marginally overshadows his ability to make deep dives into obscure information and flip it for his benefit.

He remembers their first day together, spending the week in orientation learning about Soto Labs and its purpose, pipeline, and security measures. Tyler was just an associate accountant then, earning his due over the years just as she had, to eventually become a senior accountant. He'd never forget the way she laughed in that soft, tinkling way and how her eyes lit up whenever she regaled him with tales of her family and old friends. She once told him of her special emotional connection with music, a fact he keeps in his back pocket, among other bits of information for future manipulation tactics. Tyler chooses, however, to ask her to lunch rather than play with her head today.

For a time, Abby occasionally had lunch with him when she was working on the floor. After taking the apprentice role, however, she has since become a ghost to him, with only rare morning greetings when he happens to catch her. Instead of being able to meet up with her in person, he's been relegated to watching her activities online, as well as casually striking up conversations with her lab mates as they pass through. Ben is someone Tyler tends to run into more frequently as a fellow early bird. He thinks of Ben as a tough nut to crack regarding all things social. The others, however, are even tougher. Only Abby is soft and pliable.

Tyler pecks at his keyboard to boot up Giselle, his pristine computer with the newly released Mag 9 holo monitor.

"Good morning, Tyler," the sing song and soft feminine computer voice rings out while strings of code quickly scroll up the monitor. Despite having a mild, stalker-ish obsession with Abby, he hasn't considered asking her out for whatever reason.

"Good morning, beautiful," he flirts back to Giselle while continuing to peck at the keyboard to log in.

Tyler embeds the fingers of his right hand into a palm-size black gel-like controller and wiggles them around to open the various programs on his desktop. He knows computers well, navigating the interface like a professional hacker. He considers setting a reminder for 8:50 a.m. so he can time his coffee trip to run into Abby when she comes in for the day. This is when he'll make his move to ask her to lunch. Even though Tyler has chosen to use a more chivalrous manner to attempt convincing Abby to happy hour, that doesn't stop him from rummaging through her cyber trail and seeing what she has been up to.

He credits himself for landing Abby that role downstairs. His management of that department's materials budget and his flirtatious conversations with the previous human resources specialist afforded him a particular prestigious reputation with those who matter. There had been a one-off happy hour Abby showed up for where she divulged to Tyler—after he plied her with many drinks—her dissatisfaction with her repetitive testing role and her plans to work her way up. Little did she know at the time that her open conversation with him had started the process of her moving down, which is even better. Tyler had put a lot of work into buttering up that HR hag. After landing the position for Abby, the specialist's usefulness came to an end, and Tyler's presence in her office dwindled every week until she ultimately left the company.

"Today is Friday. Happy Friday, Tyler," Giselle's voice calls out as he opens the calendar to set his reminder. He winks and clicks his tongue at the computer and begins opening all his programs for the day, including the special program he was able to install on Abby's computer without anyone knowing. This program connects directly to her computer camera. That computer, Frankie, is such trash that she isn't aware whether her camera even works. Luckily for Tyler, it does, and she doesn't bother covering it. The other unique feature of his program is it allows him to view a copy of her screen and see what she's working on.

After he opens the program and sees nothing but black, it won't be until after 9 a.m., when she's at work, that he can begin spying in earnest. In the meantime, he checks any remnant of her activities from the day before. He wiggles his fingers around in the gel of the black trackball and opens the program that recorded her screen activity.

Ah, another new invention. Let's see what it is, shall we? Reading the screen, he makes out the Animate program and its output. He eyes the red error markings following the final activation sequence. *Another failed prototype. Better luck next time.*

He squints at the name and silently mouths the word *Me-tax-ism* when he's interrupted by the silhouette of a small, stocky bald man at his door.

"Oh, hey, Nick." Tyler suppresses his surprise and quickly hits the escape key. "You're here early?"

"Is that a question?" Nick smirks as he sucks on his water bottle.

"Not at all. I'm just surprised to see anyone here this early on a Friday."

"I want to bounce out of here early, so I came in early. What are you up to?"

"Not much, just checking on a few things." He spies his screen from the corner of his eye to make sure the screen recording is gone. It is.

"Another happy hour tonight?"

Tyler does *not* want Nick to go to happy hour. He is a braggart and a buzz kill.

"Er, maybe... It's not set in stone yet, but there is some talk."

"Hm, yeah, I would go, but I have other plans." Nick takes another swig of his bottle and checks his watch.

You weren't invited. Tyler's thought is more snide than the cheerful expression on his face reflects. He's good at masking himself.

"Bummer."

"Yeah, I've had these plans for a while now." Nick sighs with an air of importance and a fish for a response.

Oooh, you're so important—you have plans. Tyler's brain is annoyed.

"Well, have fun," Tyler responds, turning his back on Nick to focus on Giselle. He can sense the heat from Nick's ire on his back for a moment before his human presence finally disappears.

Jackass. That was close, Tyler.

He makes a mental note to remind himself to ask Abby if she's created any inventions lately. He hopes to pry more information about this *Me-tax-ism* failure.

"Thanks for bringing in doughnuts!" Nick's muffled shout from a mouthful of the pastry rings from the accounting common area.

"Ugh..." Tyler softly groans, then smiles and shouts, "No problem!"

The morning couldn't drag on any slower for Tyler as he awaits his reminder. When the clock turns over to 8:50, he practically leaps out of his chair, grabbing his tried and true university mug to make his way to the atrium, then the common break area. Luck is on his side today as he sees Abby in the foyer, badging into the atrium. The door swings open, and he smells her perfume waft in, like sweet citrus and salt water. He waves at her.

"Hey, Abby!" His voice cracks a little, with an uneven tone. *Don't get too excited now.*

She looks up at him with her doe eyes. Her wavy chestnut hair is pulled back into two cute, identical messy buns under her ears.

"Oh, hey, Tyler. What's up?" she responds distractedly, fumbling around with her badge and searching the side of her bag for something. Her perfume is intoxicating, stinging the back of his mouth as if he'd eaten something sweetly sour and making him salivate. Tyler eyes her up and down in an instant during her distraction. She's casual today, wearing a flattering black V-neck and jeans with low-cut flat sneakers. A small shimmering opal rests in the dip of her neck like a hammock and is fixed by a delicate gold chain. He loves it when she dresses retro.

"Not much, just about to go get coffee. Do you have time to walk over with me?" He reasons that the common room is only a few yards away and hopes upon hope that she'll accept.

Abby quickly looks down at her watch. "Yeah, sure, I have time." *Yes! Time to be smooth.*

The pair stroll past the reception desk to the alcove behind.

"Hey, you know what I miss?" Tyler asks during their brief walk.

"What's that?"

"It's been a while since we've had lunch together..." He trails off to look at her so she can finish his thought for him.

"Yes, it has," she says, "but you know how B6 is. It's hard to get out of there for any decent amount of time."

They approach the counter, which has a large coffeemaker with two full pots and a fancier espresso machine next to it. Tyler decides to buy time with the espresso machine.

"It's Friday. There can't possibly be a whole lot going on that you couldn't step away for an old friend?" He slowly packs the coffee into the filter while biting his lower lip and gazing at her with saucer-size eyes. He sees Abby thinking about it.

"Well, Tony mentioned yesterday that he plans on showing us his new gadget today, but I'm not really sure when. I can't pass up the opportunity to learn about that prat's invention. Cocky bastard he is." Abby grimaces, sucking air in through her teeth, "Sorry, I shouldn't have said that."

"Oh, you don't like Tony?" *Pocket that, Tyler.*

"Not particularly. He's always so awful to me."

"How so?" Tyler stalls while slowly connecting the filter to the espresso unit.

"It's hard to explain... He's just always had it out for me since I started. Claims I slept my way down there."

Whoops. Tyler remembers the HR specialist's accusation against him after Abby got the role. A rumor spread quickly, but he was fortunate enough to massage that rumor to eager ears, conveniently leaving his name out of it. He shakes his head with a *tsk*.

"Men are pigs." He smiles at her. She smiles sweetly back at him, a small dimple forming at the left corner of her mouth.

"At least Tony is. I'm not technically invited to his show-and-tell, but I'm going to crash it anyway. If he does it early enough, I'll make my way up here for lunch. How about that?"

"That would be awesome! And screw Tony." The espresso sputters the last of its cycle, and Tyler takes his mug out from the machine, leaving the filter for the next person to clean.

"Hey, I have always kind of wondered..." Abby turns on her heel to look at Tyler. "Why do you always come to the common area for coffee? Doesn't the accounting area have its own kitchenette?"

"I like the espresso machine, and we don't have one over there," Tyler lies.

She silently appraises him with a half-smile that still showcases that little dimple. She looks down at her watch again.

"Well, I've got to get down there. It takes a while to move through the worm," she says after a short pause.

"The what now?" He raises an eyebrow.

Abby waves her hand to erase what she said. "You know, the steel rings."

"You call it the worm?"

"That's what it makes me think of. Chuckling, she checks her watch again.

"You'll have to tell me what that's like sometime."

"It's nothing special. Like I said, if Tony is done by noon, I'll meet you up here, and we can have lunch. Cool?"

"Cool." Tyler turns back to the accounting area as Abby moves toward the elevators. He turns again to watch her momentarily before returning to his office.

Abby makes the familiar descent into B6, passing through the worm and entering the main landing. Tony is already standing at the center, activating the small lab bench, which ascends through the mosaic floor and comes to a rest. She stops suddenly as the two lock eyes. Tony sneers and walks toward the break room to gather his intended audience. Abby rolls her eyes and follows him to the break room to drop off her lunch.

As she opens the door, Tony is already coming back out again, and he bumps into her shoulder as he pushes through. Ben stands there looking at her, wide-eyed and furious. She shrugs at him and puts her lunch away. Ben and Byron trail Tony out into the open area. Abby isn't far behind, intent on crashing Tony's show-and-tell.

Well, I suppose I can meet Tyler for lunch after all.

Ben and Byron drag heavy feet toward the lab bench in the central area while Tony is seen in his little lab window bouncing around and gathering things with a toothy grin, making Abby want to sock him in the mouth.

She approaches the two men at the lab bench. "Is Jon out today?" she asks.

"Yeah, he took a long weekend," Ben answers.

"Why do you suppose he wants to show everyone his gadget before taking it to the board?" Abby nods in the direction of Tony's lab.

"Who knows?"

Byron shrugs with a slight frown. He looks down and shakes his head.

"What's that supposed to mean?"

Byron pauses for a moment, "I can only guess as to why, but this has happened before when he—"

Tony bursts out of his lab, interrupting Byron and holding a small white box. Byron stops and stares as Tony approaches while wearing a wide grin. Abby swears, and the grin becomes even wider once he catches her standing there with the other two.

"Check it out," he begins, putting the box on the table. "Can you guess what it does?"

Ben tilts his head back and forth, observing the little white box set in a silvery frame with a fist-size hole in the side. Abby sees that the box is actually kind of pretty. Although primarily white, it resembles a large moonstone, with faint milky colors reflecting from the surface. There are five little raised nubs on the top that Abby thinks might be buttons. Also, on the surface appears to be a small LED readout screen.

Impatient with Tony's question, Byron shrugs while the little balding man looks back and forth expectantly between Byron and Ben, completely ignoring Abby.

Ben finally speaks. "It looks pretty neat, Tony, but I don't think any one of us can guess what it does. Kinda looks like a fancy alarm clock."

Tony cackles. "Oh, it does way more than just tell time! Here, put your fist into the hole."

Ben hesitantly slides his balled-up hand into the hole. Once Ben's hand is inside, Tony presses one of the buttons. After a closer look, Ben sees the buttons have little engravings on the top: from right to left is a triangle, an *H*, a *D*, a *W*, and finally, a square. Tony presses the little *H*, and the LED screen lights up blue with the number 1.

"Okay, now put your other hand on the table," Tony continues.

Ben spreads his long fingers over the black surface, his pale hand in stark contrast. Before any of them can react, Tony whips out a small blade, crudely fashioned out of one of the red metal panels all inventors carry in their lab inventory, and slashes the top of Ben's hand.

"What the hell, Tony?!" Ben's hand twitches wildly; then he rips it away from the bench, taking his other hand out of the box to hold up the injured one.

Byron grits his teeth and balls up his fists, ready to rip out Tony's throat, while Abby gasps and puts her hand to her mouth. Chuckling, Tony attempts to pry Ben's box hand from the injured one.

"Sorry, Ben. Please just put your hand back in the box and the other on the table."

Ben glares back up at Tony, his limbs rigid and unmoving.

"No, for real. I have to show this to you..." Tony continues to coax Ben's hand back toward the box. After a moment, Ben complies and slowly loosens his grip on the injured hand, blood imprinted on his palm. He balls it back into a fist as if trying to hold on to the blood that leaked from his other hand and slides it back into the pure white shimmering box. The LED still glows its little blue number one, with a tiny *H* next to it blinking slowly.

Ben places his pale hand back on the black counter. The gash is curved and split wide down the center. Wet redness lines the wound, with a messy palm print covering the surface of his hand. Gravity causes more blood to drool from the deep cut.

"Hurry up," Ben hisses through his teeth. "You probably hit a vein."

Tony returns a contemptuous smile and presses the button marked with a small triangle. The little *H* stops flashing, and the inside of the box lights up blue, reflecting off Ben's fist.

After a few seconds, Ben tilts his head again and sucks air through his teeth.

"It's getting hot," he says.

"Just wait," Tony replies.

"It's getting really hot..."

"Wait."

Ben grinds his teeth silently as they all observe the curved wound on his other hand begin to quiver. His fingers twitch again, knuckles cracking and twisting unnaturally. The room is dead with anticipation, hypnotized by the rippling slash. The light emanating from the box emits an ambient buzz that, although quiet, fills the air with a white din. The skin closes quickly as if the slash Tony performed had moved in reverse. The wound has completely closed, leaving nothing but the bloody palm print over the top.

Perplexed, Abby looks at Tony. Was this not the very same concept Ben showed her just the day before? How did they both come up with the same idea at exactly the same time? Ben seems to be thinking the same thing, and he looks immediately over to Abby, his expression screwed up into one of concern.

The light from the hole flickers off, taking the ambient hum with it.

"You can take your hand out now," Tony says, beaming at Ben.

Ben pulls his fist out quickly and traces the surface of his other hand with his index finger. He turns that hand over to see the smashed imprint of blood from a wound that never existed. He remains silent, his eyes cast down at the white box. Abby moves over to Ben to examine his wound hand, turning it back and forth in her own.

"You see," Tony begins, "it actually turns back time on your wound! I added the buttons here for hours, days, and weeks." As he speaks, he points to the three buttons with their respective letters —H, D, and W.

"For you, Ben, I just set it for one hour since I knew I was going to slash you." He laughs at the slash remark.

Abby desperately wants to gouge out his putrid, mocking eyes. She chews her lower lip with a glare that could kill him. She puts

Ben's hand down and crosses her arms. Tony takes no notice of her and continues to talk.

"This triangle is the start button, and this square is the stop button. It only goes back to at most ninety-nine weeks, which is good for injuries up to almost two years!"

Ben grunts while Byron stands still, hands stuffed in his pockets. Abby waits for him to finish.

"This could revolutionize the health industry! See, I *told* you it was clinical." He looks at Abby and scoffs. She smiles sarcastically back at him.

"I bet people would pay a ton of money to set this baby to ninety-nine weeks." Tony raps his fingers on the top of the box. "I mean, it would basically stop aging. And look, it's even big enough for your fat, meaty hand, Byron! Do you want to give it a go too?"

Tony laughs a hearty laugh alone. Byron stares back, wearing a perturbed expression that scares Abby.

"I don't think so, Tony." Byron's voice is a deep growl that can be felt in their chests.

Abby uncrosses her arms and gently places a hand on Ben's shoulder. He dips his head even lower for a second before lifting it back up and looking Tony directly in the eye.

"Good job, Tony." Ben pulls in a deep breath and closes his eyes, "This is indeed pretty cool."

Tony puffs up his chest and smiles wide, looking to Byron for more affirmation. Byron looks at him for a few seconds before turning his back on him to walk away.

"Do you think it's ready to show?" Tony looks back to Ben. He clasps his hands and bounces like a child waiting for Daddy's approval.

"Sure, I suppose. It'll probably beat Graviton."

Abby chokes in a breath, continuing to glare at Tony, knowing that each word of praise Ben offers is a gut punch.

"Great! That's awesome!" Tony grabs his box and holds it to his chest, "Since Jon is out today, I may wait until Monday. I'm so excited! Happy Friday!" He holds his head up and turns back toward his lab.

Silence fills the room until Tony's lab door closes completely.

Abby looks over to Ben. "I'm sorry." Her face dissolves into pity.

Ben stares down at his once-wounded hand, flexing and constricting it into a fist. He takes a deep breath and speaks at last. "It's not your fault. He just beat me to it."

"But how did you two come up with the same exact idea at the same time?"

Ben shrugs. "Just stupid bad luck, I guess."

Even though Abby finds Tony repugnant, she can't deny that his gadget is better than Ben's. Not only does it look like a high-class piece of jewelry, but it also can control how far back the healing should go. Almost as if Ben can read her thoughts, he silently turns to go to his lab. Alone in the core, Abby decides to also head to her lab.

Once inside, she looks around at all the different pieces of equipment and materials, feeling disheartened at all the vast possibilities they offer, yet Tony has managed to create something on the heels of Ben. As her eyes zero in on the white panels hanging innocently on their pegs, she suddenly becomes annoyed at them. She trudges over to her office and sits down hard on the chair before turning back and forth on the swivel while biting a nail. Looking at the clock, she sees only an hour has passed since she arrived at the scene of Tony's display.

Two hours, and I'll meet Tyler. I need to get out of this sour atmosphere.

Chapter 4

LUNCH

AFTER PIDDLING AROUND WITH a few ideas and still coming up empty-handed, Abby checks the clock to see that it's close to noon. Pondering Tony's gadget, she heads to the break room, gathers her lunch, and then heads upstairs to meet Tyler. She doesn't particularly care to meet Tyler, but it gives her something to do rather than look at Tony's smug face and try to console Ben secretly.

She turns to the common area to find Tyler already waiting for her, a broad, toothy grin plastered on his chiseled features. She smiles a little at that.

"Let's go somewhere instead. It's on me!" Tyler points at the door. Abby looks down at her little flowery lunch bag and shrugs. Not in the mood to argue, she puts up a finger for Tyler to wait while she runs to the common area to throw her lunch into the refrigerator.

"Where do you want to go?" she says, jogging back to Tyler in the atrium.

"Oh, there's a place not too far once we hit the main road. I can drive too."

"Sure, it'll be fun," Abby says. She is not sure if it will actually be fun, but spending time away from the stuffy atmosphere of B6 is a welcome change.

The pair step outside into the blaring sunlight, waves of heat crashing over their faces as they head to Tyler's sleek red Supra.

"Here we are." He beckons her to the passenger side, opening the door for her. Abby appreciates the chivalry but watches him warily as he practically skips to the driver's side. *I hope he doesn't think this is a date...*

He hops into the seat, and the engine roars to life. He smiles at her with a look that says he hopes she'll be impressed by it. The car is hot and stuffy from the summer heat. Rather than being impressed, she smiles back, holding in the fact that she can't breathe in there.

"Ready?" Tyler turns his attention to the dashboard, poking at various buttons until the radio kicks on and a song from The Police comes through. Abby has a bittersweet fondness for the band. Her best friend in high school once left a voice message on her phone that played "Every Little Thing She Does is Magic" until the timer quit. Remembering that suddenly makes her sad. Lee was sending her a message through that voicemail that she didn't understand until it was too late.

Tyler peels out of the parking lot, kicking up dust and making way for the narrow road leading out from Soto Labs to the main drag. Abby remains silent as the music pumps on the radio, remembering Lee and how they met. The conversation between them was juvenile but appropriate, as they met in junior high school. He was kind to her in a cold classroom where she didn't know anyone. They instantly hit it off.

"Do you like Hibachi grills?" Tyler shouts over the music.

Abby's daydream breaks, and she jumps slightly, leaning her ear closer. "What?" she shouts back.

Tyler chuckles and turns down the volume.

"I said, do you like Hibachi grills?"

"Are those the ones where you sit with other people, and the cook is there in front of you juggling rice and eggs?"

"Exactly. Ever been?"

"Can't say I have. I like rice, though, so it should be good, I think."

"Awesome, awesome... There's a really good one not far."

Abby nods and turns to look back out of the window, still distracted by thoughts of Lee. They'd drive for hours together, just talking about nothing and smoking cigarettes. Now, she's sitting in the passenger seat next to a man who's trying way too hard.

Lee taught her how to drive a stick shift in his beat-up junker, and it ended up being a challenging test. A test that ultimately would make her a skilled pro at the stick shift in a better car. Abby notices that Tyler's vehicle is a stick. He jams the stick to second, then third, as he rips through the private drive, the engine growling with the pace. He looks over at her, smiling again. The song turns over to another one that Abby recognizes and is tied to her connection with Lee.

"Oh, I love this song!" she tells Tyler and reaches to turn up the volume without his permission. His good mood allows her this courtesy.

The song fills her head once again with memories of Lee. She listens to half of the nostalgic song before turning down the volume.

"I went to a concert once where *this* band, you know, Majesty Crush, was playing with a bunch of other bands," she tells Tyler as the song continues in the background, "When they were done, they set up a booth where you could get their autograph. My friend and I went to their booth, and I swear the bassist was flirting with me."

"Really?" Tyler raises an eyebrow.

"Yeah." She sighs, remembering the moment. "I think the lead singer put in his two cents too, but I can't be sure. My friend used to tease me about it for years."

"Used to tease you? Are you no longer friends?"

Abby regrets treading into this territory, but rather than attempt to distract him away from the topic, she spills the beans.

"Yeah, we had a falling out in college. That was a long time ago."

"I'd love to hear about it," Tyler suggests as he rounds into the parking lot of the little restaurant. Abby sees a bright neon sign in the window that says "Kyoto Hibachi." He stops the car and hops out quickly to run to Abby's side and open the door. *This is very kind of him...too kind.*

Once inside, Tyler asks for a table for two instead of sitting at the grill with eight other people. Abby raises an eyebrow but goes along with it. She checks her watch, wondering if B6 would care whether or not she takes a more extended lunch. *Jon isn't here today, so whatever.* She shrugs and follows the waitress with Tyler.

They sit at a two-seater where Abby is forced to look at Tyler directly in the face.

"I thought we were going to sit at the grill? Water, please," she says to the waitress.

"Same," Tyler echoes. When the waitress leaves, he looks right at her. "So tell me about this friend of yours. What happened?"

She pauses to think about what to say. *How do I tell him about a situation like that when he probably thinks we're on a date?*

"Well," she starts, "it's embarrassing."

"Bah, I'm interested! No judgment." He puts his hand over his heart as if swearing an oath to her. She eyes him.

"Okay, he was my best friend since seventh grade. We did everything together, and I *loved* him so much." She emphasizes love to dissuade Tyler in a slightly passive-aggressive move.

"Loved?" Tyler appears to turn green.

"Well, not like that. He was like a brother to me. Like I said, we did everything together—attached at the hip practically."

"Let me guess, he loved you as more than just a sister."

"Yeah, you could say that." Abby sighs.

The waitress drops off two glasses of water. Tyler orders a noodle bowl and then looks at Abby. She quickly runs a finger down the menu and tells the waitress she'll have the same.

Tyler cocks his head at her. "Do you like octopus?" he asks after the waitress scurries off with their orders.

"What?"

Tyler laughs. "That's the noodle bowl I ordered!"

"Oh, my God..." Abby goes pale.

"Don't worry, the rest of the bowl is good. If you don't like the octopus part, I'll eat it." He gives her a handsome, toothy grin, making her blush a little.

Stop that, she orders herself.

"So what's his name?"

"Huh?" Abby forgot herself at the ordering mishap.

"Your friend—what's his name?"

"Oh... It's Lee. I think he married some chick he worked with. I haven't spoken to him since college."

She runs a finger down the side of her glass, loosing a cascade of condensation down the side. To reminisce over Lee makes her uncomfortable, and she can think of a thousand other things she'd rather talk about.

"So what did he do to end your friendship?"

Abby looks up at him and twists her face into a grimace. "What makes you think it wasn't me?"

"How could it possibly have been you?" He winks at her.

She chuckles a little at the flirtatious undertone of the wink. "Women can kinda be trash too, you know..."

"Tsk, maybe, but I can't see you as trash. Especially the kind that destroys a long friendship."

"No, I wouldn't do that. I still blame myself, though."

"So... what happened then?"

Abby considers her story. "Well, you know how I told you he was like a brother to me? I mean, we grew up together, discovered things together, and found ways to spend time together. At one point, I even dated his best friend in high school with his blessing."

"I could see how that would give you mixed signals," Tyler adds.

"Of course it did! But I messed up. I developed a small crush on one of his other friends in college."

"How is that your mistake?"

Abby shrugs. "I should have known Lee felt that way about me. The signals were there the whole time."

"How so?"

"It's hard to explain, but having known him so long, I can see it clearly, looking back. Anyway, I told him about my crush, and he confessed his love for me. After all those years! I'm actually a little mad about it. And sad. I don't know how to feel."

Tyler puts his hands over Abby's small fists on the table. "It's not your fault. How could you possibly know?"

Abby looks down at Tyler's mitts covering her hands. Her heart thumps in her chest, and she feels her face flushing. She slowly withdraws her hands from underneath his and puts them in her lap, feeling her sweaty palms and the lingering warmth from his show of affection.

"I-I didn't mean anything by that," Tyler stutters.

Abby waves her hand in front of her face. "Don't worry about it," she lies, straightening up in her chair.

Tyler clears his throat, "So what happened after that?"

"Well, this is where I really messed up. I thought about giving him a chance even though I didn't feel that way about him. I was stuck, like I didn't want to lose him as a friend if I rejected him, so I gave in to him."

"What did you do?"

"It's embarrassing."

Tyler puts his hands up. "Remember, no judgment here."

The waitress stops at their table to drop off their bowls. Abby looks down to see intact little sleeping octopi resting on the noodles. She stares for a long time at the tentacles.

Tyler laughs again, picking one up and putting it in his mouth. "Just try one."

She prods the little creature and picks it up. She gives it a squeeze. "It feels rubbery," she tells him. He nods at her to put it in her mouth. Slowly, she brings it to her face while eyeballing Tyler, then stops.

"No, I don't want to. I'm weird about textures." She puts the octopus back on its bed of noodles.

"Ah, it's all good," Tyler says as he uses his chopsticks to grab each of them from her bowl and put them in his.

If Abby's lessons with Lee had taught her anything, she knew she shouldn't feel obligated to do something beyond her comfort zone out of guilt.

"No offense," she says.

Tyler puts his hands up again. "No offense taken." His voice is clear despite the several bites of food tucked into his inner cheek. He smiles at her again, careful not to show the food in his mouth, but manages a particular kind of charm that Abby can't help but notice.

Maybe his crooked nose isn't so bad after all.

"So what did you do then? I mean, with Lee."

Abby sighs and pokes at the noodles. She purposely puts a wad of them into her mouth to avoid answering the question right away. Tyler is unrelenting and continues to eat, peering at her every few seconds to wait for her response. Abby hadn't expected the noodles to be spicy. Little beads of sweat swell on her upper lip as she watches Tyler devour the same noodles without so much of a wince. She lets out a gasp and takes a large gulp of water.

"These are hot," she coughs out.

"Yep. But does it at least taste all right?"

"Mm-hm," she mumbles. While she does like the occasional spicy dish, this one has reached a level of magma she didn't anticipate.

"You don't have to tell me what happened," Tyler says. "It's clear you don't really want to talk about it."

She sighs again. "It's just that I let him take advantage of me a little, is all. It's not like me to do that, and I'm ashamed about it. I don't like thinking about how I could have done things differently. I still dream about him."

"Did you...." Tyler raises his eyebrows suggestively.

"No! No, nothing like that." Abby's cheeks flush hot with embarrassment and spicy noodles.

"Hm, well, at least you didn't go that far. Don't be so hard on yo urself... What's done is done, and you shouldn't allow this situation to take up valuable real estate in your head."

"You're right, I suppose." She says.

Only that I still dream about him and wonder if there was anything I could have done differently.

"What did I tell you earlier?"

"Hm...?"

Tyler pauses. "Men are pigs."

"I don't think *you* are, though."

"Maybe not yet. Maybe you don't really know me...yet." He gives her another suggestive look, wagging his eyebrows.

Stop that. There is sort of an off-beat charm about him, though.

She looks back at him with a cropped smile, revealing that tiny dimple again.

The pair continue their lunch, talking about Abby's time in B6, Tyler's rise within the ranks, Abby's love for painting, and Tyler's cooking skills. Occasionally, Abby checks her watch, wondering what Ben is doing and what he has planned for the evening.

"You should definitely come to happy hour tonight," Tyler suggests, placing his credit card down for the waitress.

Abby eyes it. "You don't have to—"

"Nope, like I said, my treat! I know how hard the work can be down there, and you deserve it. Just like you should unwind with us tonight."

"I don't know..."

"Should I beg?"

She chuckles and shrugs. "Maybe you should?"

"Pu-leeese? It'll be fun!" He clasps his hands in front of him in a beggar's pose.

Abby considers her stereotype of the wild crew attending these gatherings. She wonders if his persistence involves coercing her to go home with him.

"Can I bring someone?" she says at last.

Tyler bristles. "Like who?"

"I was thinking about bringing my coworker Ben. He's had a rough day, and I think it would be good if he also unwinds."

Tyler remembers Ben. His nose forms deep wrinkles; Abby can't tell if they're from contemplative disgust or if there's an itch inside his nose that he wouldn't dare prod with a finger.

"Yeah, sure, why not? Who am I to begrudge a fellow worker from letting their hair down?" His finger strays to the top of the card as if he's second-guessing his motivation to pay. The waitress comes by and snatches it before the finger touches down.

"He's just a friend. I feel kinda bad for him," Abby blurts out, hoping to prevent any work drama and stay Tyler's jealousy.

"What happened today that's so horrible for him?"

Despite the secrecy surrounding lab activities, Abby tells Tyler about Tony Donnola and his gross display of ego that morning.

"I mean, the guy is a jerk. I told you that this morning, I think."

"Yes, you did. I'll have to look into this Tony a little more. Sounds like he doesn't belong down there with you guys."

Tyler's response surprises Abby. *Does he have some kind of pull at Soto?*

"Well, I wouldn't go that far. In the end, people like him always get what they deserve."

"If you say so." Tyler shrugs and drops the topic.

The waitress returns with the receipt, and Abby rechecks her watch. She's been gone for an hour and a half, and Tony is likelier to notice than the others and make a big deal about it.

In the atrium, Tyler thanks Abby for letting him take her to lunch. "Think about happy hour. Let me know if you decide to come."

He's really pushing this.

"So where are you meeting then?" she says, cocking her head.

"There's a place in the same square where we had lunch. It's called the Chrysalis Lounge. We're meeting around four thirty."

"Okay, I'll let you know then." She nods and turns with a wave.

Abby makes her way back to the B6 labs. *Maybe he's not so bad after all. I could see myself hanging out with him more often.* A smile creeps across her face as she imagines her world with Tyler in it.

She daydreams through the worm and into the central clearing, where Tony displayed his version of the Knitting Sphere earlier that day. Ben is standing there, leaning over the lab plinth with his cheek melting into one palm and rolling something under his other palm back and forth, his gaze cast into a void.

Abby approaches him. "Hey, Ben."

"You smell like fried noodles," he states, peering up at her and continuing to roll the object under his palm.

"Oh, I thought the worm would remove that smell," she says, looking back toward the metal corridor entrance.

She lifts a corner of her sleeve to sniff it. "Nah, just radiation. Where did you go?"

Abby tells him.

"That guy?" Ben huffs and props his face back against his palm while continuing to fidget.

"He's not so bad." Abby walks closer to him. "In fact, he wants you to come to happy hour tonight."

"Ha, that's a lie."

"Well, *I* want you to come. And he says you should come too."

"I don't know. I have a lot of thinking to do."

"Forget about that weasel. Knitting Sphere is awesome, and I think you're brilliant!"

Her words fly over his head, filling the air with empty white noise.

"I've been working on this thing for too long, and he just magically has some fantastic gadget that happens to do the same thing as mine? No, not the same...better!"

"I hate the guy just like the next person. Do you think he's up to no good?"

Ben shrugs. "I don't know. He has enough patents to put any of us to shame."

"Yeah, but most of them are goofy. I mean, a cup that can transform any liquid inside into apple juice? What's the use in something like that?"

"A patent is a patent."

Abby sighs. The badge of earning a patent is not taken lightly by her coworkers. No matter how simple, if one is granted a patent, the others will envy it. She suppresses her own jealousy whenever another inventor achieves a patent. Quality over quantity is her philosophy.

"You shouldn't look at it like that," she says.

"And how *dare* he slice my damn hand? Jon will hear about this."

"As he should!" Abby nods.

"I'm just pissed."

"I can totally understand that." Abby puts her hands on the bench, close to his, in a gesture of solidarity, "Will you just come to happy hour? It might help your anger."

Abby bites her lip and looks up at him, pleading, knowing full well that her ask is entirely selfish, wanting the company of a friend to staunch Tyler's potential advances.

"I'll think about it, I guess." He moves away from her, stuffing whatever he had been fidgeting with in his front pocket. He turns his back to Abby and returns to his lab.

At least Tony didn't see me come back in.

Her thoughts are cut short by a pair of beady eyes staring through the window from Tony's lab door.

nerves

BROKEN DOWN AND BEATEN, Ben lumbers through his lab. His head sags while he watches his feet carry him, and he pats his pocket to the rhythm of his footsteps toward where he stowed the sphere away. While he rambles through the lab, his mind rages about the time he lost working on the Knitting Sphere. He could never show his gadget now, as he might be accused of intellectual theft. Ben's feet carry him to the front of the bench where all his metal panels hang; several red ones are missing from their pegs.

"Idiot!" he shouts at the panels, giving them a bear swipe.

The little panels fly off the peg, scattering and echoing tinkly sounds throughout the lab. The peg itself squeaks and swings from the board until it gives up and drops to the bench in a clatter. Ben peers through his little lab chuck hole to make sure no one has heard this tantrum. Through the window, he sees the central clearing—empty except for the lab plinth still raised from earlier when Tony slashed him. Ben chuffs as he stares down at the panels, which are mostly unusable now with a dent here and a folded corner there. He picks up a panel, his blood-red reflection staring back at him.

Sliding a light finger down the deep, jagged scar on his left arm, he remembers the approaching guardrail and the crunch of glass. The screams echo in his memory...Holly again.

"Happy hour..." he huffs, chucking the red panel aside. He bends over to pick up the remaining panels, with dents and blemishes from their fall, twisting his reflection into sad monsters.

I hope I don't get in trouble for destroying property.

The thought of drowning his lousy mood in alcohol scratches at his past. Deep down, he knew they shouldn't have gotten into that car. Ben himself was several drinks deep, and Holly's fluid, careless demeanor behind the wheel suggested the same. He didn't know Holly very well—just another one of Shane's many girlfriends who'd offered to be the sober driver and failed to stay sober. With Shane in the front swaying like a jellyfish, a careless patch of wet leaves was all it took for Holly to jerk the wheel too hard.

The inertia opened the guardrail like a flower. It was only until an old invisible redwood, covered in a blanket of black cicadas, stood sentinel that the screams inside the car stopped, and the ones outside it began.

Holly's long mess of warm blond hair was twisted on the forest floor, a highlight of golden strands tangled with dead leaves and twigs. It didn't belong there—to Ben, it seemed like a mirage. One green eye flecked with brown was open and peered at him from under the brush, her jaw wide in a soundless scream.

Ben asked if she was okay, ignoring the wracking nerve pain shooting down his left arm. Shane groaned in the distance. The redness had spattered across her milk-pale cheek, and her foot was unnaturally poised at the crown of her head. It wasn't until Ben reached over to rouse her that he realized she wasn't getting up. Her head tottered unnaturally, facing the stars and rolling three feet forward. From the dented red panel, the same mouth twisted in that scream stares back at Ben. A shiver quakes up his torso.

Maybe I shouldn't leave Abby alone.

He thinks about the accident, seeing Abby's face in the woods. He couldn't leave Abby to suffer Holly's fate if happy hour heads in that direction.

For him, drinking would be out of the question. If he's lucky, he could convince Abby not to drink either. That would make it easy for them to leave whenever they wanted without waiting for the buzz to die.

Although Ben doesn't like Tyler, he's never been able to put his finger on why. His random encounters with him in the atrium have given him odd feelings he can't reconcile. Whether Abby has the same feelings about him is up for debate. *Maybe I'll ask her straight up*. They can talk about it before heading there as a condition of his attendance.

Just don't let her in.

Holly was the horrific tragedy of some random girl he didn't know, and his nightmares are occasionally colored with visions of her severed head. Shane's plunge from a twenty-story window corrupted his thoughts constantly. Sometimes, he would see himself falling from that window, with the pavement rushing ever closer before waking up in a cold sweat.

Shane's suicide note remains tucked in Ben's nightstand, unsealed, its ink fading from the envelope. His childhood friend was gone forever in a bout of sustained brain damage from that redwood. He had changed that night, and their friendship had suffered for it. Shane didn't mourn Holly's death; he couldn't even remember her name.

Ben runs a finger over his scar again. He makes sure to hide it from the world by wearing long-sleeve shirts, even in the dead heat of summer. *Why am I thinking about Shane when Tony just ruined me?*

He pulls the red sphere from his pocket and rolls it around in his fingertips. He stares at the tiny button. On his invention, there are no fancy dials to create time. There's no silver setting to make it look fancy.

Ben sighs and reconsiders happy hour, stuffing the little orb back into his front pocket. He checks his watch to see that two hours have passed since Abby returned from lunch with Tyler.

He decides to call her.

The receiver picks up, and Ben hears it clack to the floor. Muffled swishing sounds scrape his ears as Abby curses in the background.

"H-hello? Ben?"

"Hey."

"What's up? No one ever calls me," she says, laughing.

"Will you come by real quick?"

"Uh, sure! Be there in a sec."

Twenty seconds pass until Ben hears a tiny rapping on his lab window. He lets her in, and she creeps inside, trying to hide.

"Oh, who cares who sees you come in here? I don't care."

Abby straightens up and frowns as Ben turns his back and heads toward his office.

"Did you hear that crashing noise earlier?" Abby says, her eyes moving toward the floor. A scattering of red panels are strewn over the tile.

"Oh," she says, widening her eyes and holding her breath.

Ben ignores her and motions for her to come into the office. She settles into the spare chair, looking at him with a waiting smile.

"Did you say you had a prototype?" he asks.

"Yes." She points a finger in the air in triumph. "But I will only show you at happy hour."

Ben rolls his eyes.

"Stop that." She pushes his shoulder.

"Okay, I'll come to your precious happy hour. Will you stop asking now?"

"Yes, I will." She crosses her arms and smiles.

"You really shouldn't bring a prototype outside the lab. It's technically Soto's property."

"Frankie screwed it up. It's a dud anyway. It's more like a pretty paperweight at this point."

Ben looks at her from the corner of his eye. "Who put Frankie together?"

"Hm? Frankie? I dunno. Why?"

"Just curious. It's unusual that the Animate dock will screw up an activation."

"Yeah, well, this one did. My prototype is kinda pretty, though, so I'm excited to show you."

Ben nods and rubs his chin. "So what is Tyler planning for happy hour?" he says, changing the subject.

"What do you mean by that?" Abby raises an eyebrow.

"I mean, you never really want to go to these things, but now all of a sudden, you're gung-ho about it, wanting to drag me with you."

Abby frowns. "Well, if you think I'm *dragging* you—"

Ben waves his hand and shakes his head. "No, I didn't mean it like that. I'm just wondering why you want to go so bad."

Maybe because I kinda like Tyler?

"Well..." Abby stops. *No, you can't say that.* "I just thought maybe since you had a bad day and Tyler has been hounding me to go, that we could go together."

"Is he interested in you?"

"What? N-no! I mean, I don't think so." Abby rears back, knowing the truth.

Ben clicks his tongue, "Don't be naive."

"I'm not being naive."

"I just think you need to be careful. Especially around guys. Trust me, I know how they think."

"Okay, Dad," Abby rolls her eyes and smiles. *Please don't turn into Lee.*

"I'm being serious. At this point, I don't trust anyone anymore."

"What about me?"

Ben eyes her for a moment, his silence making her uncomfortable and causing her to shift in her seat. The dainty pendant she wears rocks back and forth, glinting under the lab lights as the muscles in her neck flex and relax.

Don't let her in.

"I guess you're all right," he says, smirking. "We're just friends, though."

Abby sighs, her tension relaxes, and her heart slows. She's grateful to hear Ben say that. "Well, maybe you can protect me. I might be warming up to him a little bit too."

Ben crosses his arms. They rest on a bit of belly pooch that sticks out as he sits. "Is that right?"

She pinches her thumb and forefinger together. "Maybe a tiny bit."

"I gotta tell ya, there's something off about that dude."

Abby sits upright and leans toward him. "What do you mean by that?"

Ben shrugs. "I don't really know. There's just something about him that rubs me the wrong way. It seems like I run into him every morning. Some days he's friendly; other days, he looks like he wants to slit my throat."

"Really? Does he ever talk to you?"

"On the days he's friendly, he does." Ben sways back and forth in his office chair, belly pooch wiggling under his arms.

"Well, what does he say to you?" Her interest piques with renewed vigor.

"He's only ever asked about you and what you're up to. I swear he probably still doesn't even know my name."

"Really? I'm sure he knows your name..."

"If I'm going to be honest, I think he's a little obsessed with you."

"No, that's not true. He's a nice guy!"

Ben huffs. "Just be careful, okay?"

Abby raises an eyebrow. "Sure."

"I'm definitely going with you now since you're so keen to dismiss my feelings about it."

"Don't be like that, Ben. Hey, I appreciate your concern—I do! But do you think I should go out with him if he asks me? I mean, aside from your *concerns*?" Abby bites at her thumb.

Ben glares at her. "They're concerns for a reason, Abs."

She lets out a deep belly laugh. "Abs? Did you just call me...*Abs*?"

"Yeah, so what?"

"That's what my mom calls me!" She squeezes her eyes shut and laughs again. Ben smiles, throwing his arms up.

"I guess instead of 'Dad,' I can call you 'Mom.'" She grins wide, the single dimple digging deeply into her cheek.

"You don't want me to be your mom or your dad. If I were, you wouldn't be going to that happy hour *or* seeing this Tyler fellow—you'd be marching straight up to your room and reading yourself to sleep like a good little angel."

Ben pushes a finger into Abby's shoulder as she grips her stomach, which shakes from laughter.

"Well, you'll just have to be both Mom and Dad. I'll call you 'Mad!'"

Ben wags his index finger at Abby. "Mad orders you to stay in my sight the whole time, and I'll be the judge of this guy and whether he's worthy of your time and energy."

Abby chuckles, letting the laugh draw out into a sigh.

"Where did you say this happy hour was again?" Ben asks.

"Chrysalis Lounge. Supposedly, it's not far from here."

"Of course he'd pick *that* place."

"Pardon? What was that, Mad?" Abby cracks a smile.

"Just...never mind. I think it's best if we don't actually drink anything alcoholic."

"Is there something you're not telling me?"

"No, I just think it's best if we stay sober so we can get out of there whenever we want."

Nodding, Abby nods in a way that makes her look like she's bobbing to a tune in her head. "You're right, no drinking. Pinky swear." She sticks out her pinky.

Ben rolls his eyes and hooks his little finger around hers. "Pinky swear."

"So am I just going there to order a sodey-pop?" She lays thick sarcasm over her last words.

"Or water."

Abby sighs and shakes her head with a slight smile.

"I never told you this..." Ben pauses, his look telling her of his uncertainty to say anything more.

Abby's muscles tense, and she stops rocking back and forth in her chair. Her hands are wrapped around the side of it, smashing the soft foam while waiting for him to say his piece.

"About twelve years ago, I was in an accident with a friend during a night of drinking. I strongly suggest taking it easy."

"Oh, my gosh. I'm sorry—is everyone okay?"

"No. No, they're not."

Not knowing what to say, Abby remains silent, her gray eyes staring at him.

"My best friend was in that accident," he says, "and some random girl I didn't really know. But it didn't make her fate any less tragic."

"W-what happened to her?"

"She died on the scene. I found her."

Ben stops, looking at the frown twisted on Abby's face. Right now, she looks like his mother, with deep wrinkles and frown lines spreading from the corners of her eyes. The details would probably send her into a panic, so Ben decides to leave out Holly's severed head.

"Yeah it wasn't a pretty sight, but the worst part was when my friend...left me."

"What does that mean?"

Ben looks down and smiles at his feet.

"Shane was a funny guy. Shane Mars. Knew him since grade school."

He tells her about how Shane used to be a chubby guy, the fat class clown—but it never deterred him from making friends or having girls swoon over him. He had a charm about him that Ben couldn't hold a candle to.

"When I was a kid, we had a stupid little song we used to sing about him. I don't remember the tune of it, but the words were, 'Little Shane, little Shane, boy from the stars. Tried to catch Venus but landed on Mars.' It was such a dumb song, but we used to sing it on the playground when all the girls chased him around. I swear, that's probably how he got skinny."

Abby barks out a laugh, trying not to sound unsympathetic and failing. She clears her throat and trains her face into a lamenting smile.

Ben catches the switch but continues. "High school was really good to him. I mean, really good. It's like the chub was pre-muscle waiting to harden and sculpt him into some Greek god."

He doesn't know why he's telling Abby about Shane. He never properly grieved his death, despite losing him over a decade ago, and he isn't about to start grieving in front of her. His face melts into a deep frown. The corners of his lips quiver as he looks back down at his feet, neck muscles rigid and planting his head in place.

"He was such a good friend. I was never the one people went to. It was always him. He never tossed me aside, though. He always had me there, but not like his shadow or anything. Like his equal."

He feels his eyes start to burn, knowing the grief is trying to claw its way out of his face. He won't show her this weakness. He swallows hard, hoping it'll dry up his eyes and drain his sinuses back to normal.

"*You're* the one I go to," Abby says, pointing to her chest.

Ben raises his stiff neck to swipe at his cheek, hoping his movement is fast enough to make it look like he's scratching his cheek with his palm. He huffs, a tiny crackle of snot popping in his nostril.

"Well, I'm the only one left now anyway. The accident gave Shane a weird kind of brain damage, making him paranoid and forgetful. He lived another year or so, but I guess he decided he was done. He reserved a hotel room twenty stories up and threw himself out of it."

Abby gasps and holds a hand to her mouth. Ben's words are blunt. He's no longer sugarcoating the story for her, knowing that reality is harsh and she needs to experience it. She needs to know the consequences of guys like Tyler. His tears retreat into their sockets as his face gets serious again.

"Here's my reminder of those days," he carefully unbuttons the collar of his left sleeve and rolls up the thin dress fabric.

The pale scar is glossy under the electric lights. As he turns his forearm back and forth, the wrinkles of fibroid tissue twist and squeeze, looking paper-thin. The scar is an open mouth, covering about a third of his forearm and creeping farther up his bicep. Abby can't tell how far up it goes, as he can't push the fabric up any higher, but the mouth disappears under the roll.

"I had some nerve damage, but fortunately they were able to stitch that nerve and save most of it. Thankfully, I just have a small twitch from time to time. Look, I don't want him to try anything with you."

She continues to stare at him over her fingers, raising her eyebrows. "I'm not worried about him." Her voice is muffled as she squishes her hand over her lips.

"Well, I am. Guys like that tend to take advantage of girls like you. Trust me, I know." Ben folds his shirt sleeve back over before buttoning the cuff and brushing the fabric straight.

Abby nods and lowers her hands. "Hey, I'm not so naïve anymore, I'll have you know."

She rests a small fist on her hip, cocking her shoulder to the side. "Any *more*?"

"I have my own stories to tell, but I don't know if you can handle them."

She sticks her nose up in the air, showcasing that little dimple again with an impish grin.

"Oh, I can handle anything you dish at me. Tell Mad all your secrets, young lady! Was it drinking? Drugs? Or..." He lets out a verklempt gasp. "Did you sneak out of your house after curfew?"

Ben fans himself as if to faint, and Abby giggles at his theatrics. He's thankful for the change in conversation.

"In all seriousness, though, it was none of those things, *Mad*. I just have deep trust issues with people."

Ben raises an eyebrow. *Surely she can't be serious.* He doesn't question her, but his brain screams doubt.

"Just because I have a small"—she pinches her fingers together—"teeny-tiny attraction to Tyler doesn't mean I'm open to him being a perv and taking advantage of me."

"It's more than just that, though. He's going to try to get you drunk, and I don't want to see you end up like Holly."

"I understand where you're coming from—I do—but don't worry about me... I'm glad you're coming, though."

Ben huffs, running his left hand through his hair. His hand squeezes a tuft, abruptly shaking it as if electricity is buzzing through it. He grits his teeth, then lets go when the shaking subsides.

"I always forget to stop using that hand to mess with any other part of my body," he says, rubbing the top of his head with his right hand.

"Was that one of your 'small' twitches then?" She makes air quotes around "small," seeing that nearly ripping a chunk of hair out is anything but.

"Yeah, they come and go when I don't expect them, so I try not to use this arm for much."

"I never actually noticed that, but now that I know, I won't be able to unsee that."

Ben laughs, rubbing the arm. "But seriously though, you want to end up like me?"

"Point taken, Mad. Definitely no drinking. I don't like to drink much anyway."

"You'd better not—you pinky swore."

Abby checks her watch. "Oh, crap, it's already close to five. I think I told Tyler we'd meet him at four thirty."

Ben had never set up his computer to talk to him, so it remained dead and silent with no reminder for the end of the day. Frankie is probably chittering and stammering his warning over and over in her lab. Abby could never fix him so he only said it once.

"I'm going to run back to my lab and, grab my gadget and meet you out in the center. Sound good?"

Ben nods and turns to his computer.

Abby jogs to her lab and throws open the door to hear Frankie's stuttering male-female voice shouting the time over and over.

"Yes, yes, Frankie! Shut up!" she barks, knowing he doesn't respond to voice commands.

She pushes her chair aside and hits the escape key to make him stop. The lab falls into silence, with the low hum of the HVAC system running. Metaxysm still sits on her desk where she left it. She puts it in her hand, feeling the energy on her skin and the music in her ears. She then tucks it gently into her pocket, being careful with the sharp edges, trying to prevent it from shredding her pants. The cube sits tightly against her thigh, the corners slightly digging into her skin.

She grips the cube cloaked in the fabric and pinches it outward to relieve the dig, but her pants aren't stretchy, so it continues to hug her with its teeth.

After patting all her pockets to make sure she has all her things, she turns Frankie off and heads out the door.

Still wanting nothing more than to go home and forget about today and Tony's punch in the face, Ben trudges to his car and waves at Abby.

"See you in a minute!" she shouts from the end of the lot.

He ducks into his little blue sedan, feeling a lump in his pocket.

Knitting Sphere. Oops.

If Abby knew Ben had walked out with a gadget, he'd never hear the end of it. She would think him a hypocrite.

He starts the car, listening to the engine rumble and thinking back to the sounds of the crash that took a head and a life. Holly's body was covered in wandering cicadas, oblivious to what they trod on. He can't even see one of those bug-eyed alien insects without thinking about their prickly legs, feeling Holly's dead, ghostly, pale flesh. He charges through a series of scenarios in his mind. What if he had chosen differently that night? If he had, what would his life look like now? Would he even be at Soto Labs? Would he know Abby at all? If he didn't, he knows for sure that he wouldn't be heading to Chrysalis Lounge right now—and he'd be happier for it.

He digs around in his pocket and finds the stowaway ball, briefly looking at the shining red surface before tossing it into his cup holder to deal with on Monday. It rattles around the sides and settles to the bottom. The once highly prized creation he was so proud of now sits there in its lackluster color and small profile— a tiny reminder of his inadequacy.

Chapter 6

CHRYSALIS

"It is now four o'clock. Have a good evening, Tyler," Giselle's glossy voice chimes on the hour. Instinctively, Tyler checks his watch, the hands pointing where Giselle told him they would.

He taps various buttons on the keypad, escaping out of spreadsheets and spy programs. He runs his fingers through his tousled hair, smoothing it back for better presentation. After lunch with Abby, he learned several things. For one, she hadn't done anything of use that day. After learning about her troubles with him, he also checked in on Tony's activities and background.

An interesting fact stood out to him. Tony has been spying on everyone in the lab except Jon. Tyler doesn't have explicit proof, but a suspicious digital signature lies deep in the code of Abby's machine, which he also spotted after tapping into both Byron's and Ben's computers. Jon's computer remains clean of the imprint, as does Tony's.

Abby's hatred for the man and the more significant number of patents he's "earned" puts Tony on Tyler's radar.

Unless Jon and Tony are working together. But why would only Tony have the patents? I should have protected Abby better than that. I should have watched her computer more closely.

Tyler mentally kicks himself. If Tony has the aptitude to hack into everyone else's computers and notes, he'll undoubtedly find Tyler's trail.

I haven't been caught yet, but better safe than sorry—I'll remove the software by Monday.

He rakes his fingers through his hair again, blowing out a puff of air and turning off Giselle. He plans to tell Abby about his suspicions this evening. He checks his phone for a message from her, but still nothing. He gathers his bag and slings it over his shoulder. *I hope she comes.*

He meditates over each step he takes through the accounting office toward the atrium, giving each stride ample potential to allow him to run into her on the way out.

"Hey, Ty. I'll see you there!" A bright ginger-haired intern rushes past him, three steps for Tyler's one, and waves. Tyler waves back and nods as the kid disappears through the front door.

A group of girls from purchasing approach him. One of them puts her arm around Tyler's shoulder. He smells her sweat.

"Hey, are you heading out now? We're going together. See you there!" She giggles with a vacant expression—a genuine airhead.

"See ya." He watches them go. The airhead struts toward the exit with the others. He can practically see the bottom of her fat butt with the unprofessional taupe skirt that clings to her skin. Her baby-blue top showcases the rolls squeezing from her ill-fitting bra. She reminds him of a sausage squeezed in its casing. *You don't even compare to her. Stop trying.*

He deliberately plants one foot after the other and scans the atrium—no sign of Abby. The area silences and stills as the remaining Friday stragglers exit the building. Tyler stops to recheck his phone—still nothing.

He blows air through pursed lips and taps the tip of his toe against the marble tile. *Tip-tip-tip* echoes in the empty atrium. Checking his watch once again, he strides out the door.

Chrysalis Lounge's modest parking lot is stuffed with a rainbow of cars in all shapes and sizes. It's one of the few places remaining in the state that still allows patrons to order authentic Xyloflux Spirit. Tyler angles his red Supra into a small open spot partially overtaken by the rear wheel of a fat truck tire. He squeezes from the driver's side and sidesteps from the spot.

Opening the door releases a steady stream of jocular laughter and chattering, which resonates as a clatter of cymbals and gongs to Tyler's eardrums.

"Hey, Ty! Over here!" He can only read the airhead's lips as she waves her arm from the back of the room. He can see the dark sweat pools clinging to the armpit of her light-blue top.

He walks to the table with the girls from purchasing, the ginger intern, and several other men and women from materials management. He already sees glasses of Xyloflux sitting at the table, scattered among the group.

"Yo, Ty. I already ordered you an XS." A wiry, freckled man points to Tyler and motions to a seat near him.

"Thanks, Brett! What's uuppp?" Tyler puts on his social game, sliding into the seat in between Brett and the airhead.

A waitress with a smart black-and-white blouse and hair pulled into a tight bun wanders to their table, tray poised in hand, balancing six or seven glasses. She pulls one off and hands it to Brett, who slides it over to Tyler.

The glass sloshes fat cubes of ice and an ocean-blue liquid smelling of sharp herbals. Tyler takes a small sip, breathing in with his nose and blowing out with his mouth before swallowing. A mix of grassy notes mingle with subtle blackberries and citrus, coating his throat with a warmth that reminds him of how much he adores XS.

"I'm already on my second," the airhead breathes into Tyler's ear.

"I can tell," he says, waving a hand across his wrinkled nose. She giggles and puts her arm around him, taking another sip. The wet blotch presses against his lavender button-up. Tyler sighs and rolls his eyes before taking another mindful sip.

Brett leans over to Tyler's ear and points a thumb at the airhead. "Hey, Ty, you gonna hit that again tonight?"

"Nah, bro, I've got other priorities tonight," Tyler emphasizes the last word.

"Sweet, mind if I...?"

"Go for it man," Tyler says, bringing the glass back up to his lips. *I'm going to stay pure for Abby from now on.*

The ginger intern finishes his glass, opting for water afterward.

"I gotta drive, and this stuff is messing me up." He laughs at the girl next to him.

Tyler swigs the last dredges of his glass and orders a second.

The waitress returns with his second round. He orders a third before she leaves. The first glass is making Tyler feel pretty good, loosening his muscles. He relaxes at the airhead's arm around his shoulder, no longer paying attention to her sweaty pit.

The clinking glasses, laughter, and shouting swirls in his mind, muffling in and out of focus as his head fills with cotton. He grins and puts the second glass to his lips. Letting the cool heat slide down his throat, he checks his phone again. No message.

He throws his head back in disappointment. The phone buzzes in his palm just as he swallows the last of the second glass.

> Abby: Hey, Tyler. Sorry, I got caught up in the lab. I'm on my way now.

Hell yeah. He squints at the time—it's already 5:15.

He isn't sure when the waitress came by again, but a fresh third glass sits before him.

"Dude, they cut you off at three now." The guy next to Brett stabs a finger at Tyler's glass. *Is his name Don? From materials management? Eh, Who cares.*

"I just need one more. Hey Garrett... Garrett!" The ginger intern turns to Tyler. "Can you order another XS for me?"

"Sure, man, but I'm just on waters now." Garrett is bombed, swaying back and forth and bouncing off the shoulder of the girl next to him. She's annoyed, pushing him back every time he gets close.

"No problem, my guy. I just need to bypass the cap."

Tyler swirls the full third glass over the table, watching the condensation slither over the surface of the polished wood. A rainbow of color flashes over the condensation, sparkling and fading like fireworks. *Damn, I've become a lightweight.*

Tyler looks up and watches Brett. He's talking to Don, but his lips are geometric triangles—red, pink, and orange flapping shapes. Tyler sways, circling his gaze around the table.

"Ty, are you already hallucinating? Ty. Tyler...Tyler Rowe!"

"What?" He glares at the airhead.

"I'm going to have to drive you home if you're already thrashed." She wraps her hand around his forearm and slides it down to the top of his hand.

"Whatever." He rips his arm away and rechecks his watch: 5:25.

There she is.

***

Abby strides through the front door. She cups her hands over her ears and shrinks into her shoulders at the noise. Tyler sees her turn around, her lips moving at someone behind her. *Who's that?*

Ben follows her, pulling the door closed and nodding at her moving lips. Tyler's brow sinks low toward the bridge of his nose.

I know that guy. What's-his-name. Never telling me any good stuff about Abby.

His third glass sweats large bulbous drops, running over his fingers gripped to the sides. *You can't have her.*

The waitress drops off the fourth glass next to Garrett. Once she's out of sight, he slides the glass to Tyler.

Abby sees Tyler and waves. He waves back at her wildly. *Why is she sitting at the bar?*

"I don't want to go back there," Abby tells Ben. "It's too crowded."

"It's loud in here too," he says.

"Oh, he's coming over."

***

"Hey, Abby! Hey! I got something for you." Tyler trots to Abby, nearly twisting an ankle but saving the glass from dropping to the floor.

Tyler slides Garrett's drink in front of her.

Ben stares down at the drink and back up at Abby.

"I'll be right back, 'kay?" Tyler leans back and wobbles, circling a finger. He turns around and jogs to the pack near the back.

Abby grimaces at Ben and shrugs.

"Don't drink that," Ben says, pointing at the ocean-blue liquid.

"Why? What is it?"

"XS. If you're not used to it, you'll hallucinate faster."

"Hallucinate? Why would he give me that?"

Ben folds his arms and raises an eyebrow at her.

"Yes, Mad," She smiles, poking the drink away with a finger.

"I think he's already there." Ben nods at Tyler.

***

I have to slow down a little. Tyler sees waves of heat passing over the walls and distorting the airhead's face.

"Ty, are you all right?" she asks, rubbing his arm.

He looks down at her. The tight shirt squeezes a plump cleavage. She straightens her back, and her breasts stick out, nearly bursting from their holster. Milky iridescent colors swirl over the balloons as each one breathes independently up and down, in and out. The image hypnotizes him. The feel of her hand rubbing his arm disgusts him but thrills him all the same—hairs sticking out from his neck. *Succubus.*

He imagines she's Abby rubbing his arm. The daydream fills him with warmth. He looks at her sitting at the bar with Ben, rage swelling in his gut.

"I'm not going home with you tonight," he tells the airhead, shaking her hand off his wrist, "but Brett is down for an after-party."

He nods at Brett, who's been intently listening to their conversation. Brett winks at the airhead and raises his glass.

She blushes and tucks her hands into her lap, further pushing the warbling cleavage toward Brett.

***

Abby frowns. "I swear, that's not the Tyler I met for lunch today."

"Maybe the Tyler you met was a mask, and this is who he really is," Ben says.

Abby lets out a wisp of breath. Perhaps Ben is right. Her fleeting thoughts of taking Tyler up on his advances start to dissolve.

"Well, we're here, so I'll just show you my invention while no one's paying attention."

Abby's fist writhes around in her front pocket.

"Do you not carry a purse ever?"

"No—if I carry a purse, I'm tempted to carry a ton of crap." She pokes her tongue out of the corner of her mouth as she pulls the gadget from her tight pocket. "Here it is." She lifts it between three fingers, twisting it back and forth.

The layers appear and disappear as she turns the cube. Ben leans forward and squints.

The room sways, merging colors and sounds. Tyler turns toward Abby and Ben. He puts one foot in front of the other, moving through water with cotton legs. He thinks he hears his name in the distance, but it might be in his head.

Abby has a pink halo of light around her. She smiles and talks with her hands, a feature he used to know about her when she was a biologist. His heart pumps as his wispy legs pull him toward the bar where the light shines. There's a darkness sitting next to her that threatens to swallow her light. Tyler scowls as the shadow leans in too close.

***

"I'm sorry. Am I interrupting?" Tyler glares at Ben.

Ben rears back, and Abby closes the cube in her fist, mouth mid-sentence.

"Ah, Tyler! No, um, we were talking about work, nothing fun."

"What *about* work?" Tyler sways, the drink in his grip swishing over the glass and dripping condensation in fat drops to the floor.

"Why don't you sit down?" Ben motions to a seat next to him.

"Nah, I'm good. What were you saying about work?"

Abby looks at Ben. "Um, I was just showing Ben a dud I made yesterday."

"Lemme see."

Tyler swipes at Abby's arm held behind her back.

"Tyler, stop. You're messed up." Ben reaches out to the staggering man.

"I'm *fine*. I don't need you."

Ben raises his arms and motions for the bartender.

"Lemme see," he says again, holding a hand out.

"Okay, Tyler, here. This is the dud."

Abby pulls her hand back out, showing the cube. Tyler swipes it from her, knocking his fist into her hand. He turns the cube back and forth, in awe of the disappearing layers. The metal hums low but enough for his eyes to become entranced by the cube.

"Cooool. What does it do?"

"I told you, it's a dud. It doesn't do anything."

"It feels cold. Maybe it's an ice cube!" He plunks the cube into his glass, swirling it around and gulping down a swig. He smacks his lips and sways. "Nope, my drink ain't any colder."

"Why did you do that?" Abby shrieks.

"For real...Tyler... You have no idea what you just did." Ben tries to grab the glass from him.

Wide-eyed and pressing a shaking hand against her forehead, Abby watches the men grapple at the glass. Ben succeeds in wresting it from Tyler.

Abby pokes a finger into the glass to fish out the cube, but it's even more invisible in the ocean-blue liquid.

She leans over to Ben and whispers. "Am I going to hallucinate by having my finger in here?"

"No, you're fine," he says.

Swaying stupidly, Tyler continues to watch them with a scowl. She catches the sharp corner of Metaxysm and slides it out of the glass, using the side for stability. As it rocks in her palm, she notices its-once turquoise hue has become steely gray and no longer humming.

"I don't feel good," Tyler moans. He hiccups a wet belch, putting his fist to his mouth and swallowing.

Ben sighs. "Let us take you home." He tugs on Tyler's arm.

"No!" He jerks his arm away.

"Really, Tyler, we'll drive you home," Abby pleads.

"Only if *you* drive and *he* sits in the back."

Ben rolls his eyes and nods at Abby.

"Sure, Tyler," she says. "Let's get you home."

Ben weaves through the crowd to tell the table in the back that they're taking Tyler home. Abby watches as he throws down a bill—most likely a twenty. A few patrons shake their heads and look up at Abby, who steadies Tyler by the arm. A girl in a tight light-blue blouse frowns, giving a meek wave.

Abby and Ben leave Chrysalis Lounge after only an hour. Tyler hangs between them, slung over and struggling to stand with his own strength.

"I'm sorry, Abby," he says, belching again. The scent of herbals and seaweed wafts over her, and she wrinkles her nose.

"It's all right," she says.

"It's not all right. I'm making a fool of myself."

Ben nods in agreement.

"We'll talk about it later, okay?"

"All right."

Ben props Tyler in the passenger seat of Abby's little two-door gray economy car. He jogs to the driver's side to squeeze himself into the backseat, feeling his hair brush against the ceiling before sitting low and uncomfortable.

"Sorry, Ben. It's small back there."

He gives her the thumbs-up while eyeing Tyler. His skin is pale, with drops of sweat over his forehead. While Abby gets in and messes around with the panels, the cabin fills with the stench of raw sewage and bile.

"Hey, Abby, can we hurry up?" Tyler grabs his stomach. "I'm really not feeling well."

Tyler is the source of the stench: a thick, putrid aroma of pre-diarrhea. Abby cranks the car on and peels out from her spot. Ben grapples at the window, trying to push it down.

"Abby, the window locks," he says.

Her fingers are quick to comply. Ben's hair whips around at the air now pouring into the cab. All the windows are cracked, and Ben gasps in the life-saving freshness. Tyler slumps in his seat, eyelids heavy.

"Tyler, I need your help getting to your place." Abby pushes on his shoulder.

He puts a hand to his mouth again, swallowing hard.

"Just take the in-ner belt to Ashcroft—urp. Do you know where Circle Point is?"

"Isn't that a retirement community?"

Tyler gives her a hard look of disappointment. "No! There are just a lot of old-er people—er—there."

Abby presses the gas hard, causing both men to flatten against their seats. The same sewer scent floats through the car and out the window. She loathes to have to clean up vomit, let alone watery crap.

Ben clutches the sides of his seat, feeling the velocity burn his stomach. He closes his eyes, hoping the car ride will be quick. Not wanting to reflect on his past, he tries to empty his head of all thoughts. Abby cranks on the radio to drown out the sound of whipping air that filters the smell. She takes corners and weaves through traffic, expertly watching for the law and peeking at Tyler now and then. Tyler's eyes are also closed as he grips his stomach and lets out loud belches. Ben can feel Abby hit the gas a little harder every time one of those belches hits the air.

"I'm never drinking XS again," Tyler moans. "I don't think it's ever done this to me before."

"We're almost at Ashcroft," Abby says. "Just concentrate on not pooping in my seat, please."

The exit comes fast, with the car reaching green light after miraculous green light. The neighborhood is tucked away, deep into greenery lined with expensive homes. Abby almost misses the sign for Circle Point, as it's partially hidden by towering pines surrounding the community. She pulls onto a narrow road, and Tyler's complex opens before her.

"Which building, Tyler? Hey, Tyler, which building?" She rouses him from his stupor.

"Uh, seven. Building seven."

She yanks the wheel toward building seven before screeching to a halt in front of a crescent-shaped drive.

"Do you want me to walk you to your door?" Ben offers.

"No, that's fine." Tyler belches again, struggling to get his words out.

"Okay, well, hey, get some rest, all right? Send me a message tomorrow, and I can come get you and take you back to your car," Abby says.

"Come visit me again sometime," Tyler slurs. He pulls a wadded used bar napkin from his pocket and faces Ben. "Yo, dude, you got a pen?"

Ben wafts his hand in front of his nose at Tyler's breath. He doesn't have a pen, but he sees one on the floor in the backseat.

"Here." He shoves the pen at Tyler.

Drunkenly scrawling his address on the napkin, he belches again and pushes the napkin toward Abby. His eyes are vacant and drooping.

"I'll talk to you later." Tyler rolls out of the car, catching himself well for a drunk. He takes long, quick strides toward the apartment courtyard while holding the back of his pants.

"Oh, thank God," Abby says as she gets out for Ben and surveys the passenger seat.

Ben also takes a look before sliding into the warm seat. "He should pay to fumigate your car."

Abby titters and gets back behind the wheel. She digs in her pocket for Metaxysm while pulling away from the complex.

"Did you see what happened to my gadget after Tyler put it in his glass?"

She draws the cube from her pocket and hands it to Ben, who turns it back and forth.

"It seems...different. With an odd expression, he continues to turn it.

"Yeah, it changed. It used to be a really pretty turquoise. Now it's dull and dead looking."

"I can see that. Plus, it's not humming anymore."

Abby looks at him sharply, almost taking the wheel with her and taking out a row of rosebushes.

"You could hear the humming too?"

"Of course! It was kinda nice."

Abby sits silently, biting her bottom lip in concentration. "You don't think it made him sick, do you?"

"How could it? You said it was a dud, right?"

"Well, sure, but I was only basing that off the fact that two attributes came out corrupted. I never actually tested the thing. Jerk!" Abby sticks her middle finger out at a truck that just cut her off.

"Oof, Tyler's gone now. You can calm down." Ben laughs at her rage.

"Ugh, sorry. I was so afraid he was going to mess up my seat. I don't know him well enough to spend my evening cleaning up the inside of his guts."

"That's why I told you not to drink that XS he brought you. It can do some crazy things to you."

"Are you sure, though, that this didn't make him sick?" She points at the cube still sitting in Ben's palm.

"Well, I'm not totally positive. You said there were two corrupt attributes? What were the other four?"

Abby furrows her brow. "Let me think... Excitement... Rebirth... hold on."

She counts imaginary numbers on her fingers while staring upward. A horn screams beside her when she lists over to the lane on her left. She mouths "sorry" at the driver, who shakes a wrinkled fist at her. Ben takes in a sharp breath and closes his eyes.

"Oh, Transmogrification and Passion!"

"Okay, let's see—well, if, and I *pray* if some effect was activated in his drink, Passion is probably the worst one in the bunch."

"Why do you say that?"

"Duh, Abs. I told you I think the guy's obsessed with you! I mean, if you just slapped him with more passion, I can only imagine the outcome."

Abby grimaces. "He seemed really sick, though. And the *smell*..."

"Oh, you're not turned on by the hot recesses of Tyler's large intestine?"

"Gross!" Abby chuckles.

She pulls back into the lot at Chrysalis Lounge. Earlier, she couldn't have imagined more cars being jammed in this lot, but somehow the public managed. She sees Tyler's Supra wedged in a small spot with two cars on either side of it parked on their lines and squeezing it in. Ben hands her the dead gray gadget.

"If you're worried about him..." He gets out of the car and shuts the door. Peeking through the open window, he scratches his nose, "...just check up on him tomorrow. You have his number, and now you know where he lives."

"You're right. I'm sure it's nothing." *Except my blood was inside it.*

She doesn't tell Ben about the blood. Waving and telling him she'll see him on Monday, she pulls away and disappears down the road.

With no interest in staying at the lounge, Ben crawls into his vehicle, glad the ordeal is over.

Damn, she can be so naïve.

Ben steers toward home, glad he was there for her.

I mean, who knows what would have happened to her if I hadn't been there to tell her what that drink was?

He puts a hand over his left bicep, feeling the wrinkles of his deep scar under the long-sleeve fabric. *Crisis averted.*

***

Sourness roils in Tyler's gut. Avoiding a scene, he attempts to hurry through the courtyard to his apartment undeterred. The landscape is freshly manicured, with a few sprinklers *tut-tut-tutting* over the grass. He chases up the steps toward his floor when a little old lady cracks open her door and wanders out to her lawn.

"Oh, hello, Tyler," her voice warbles.

His gut rumbles furiously. The sensation is unlike anything he's ever felt before, and he struggles to understand whether he needs to throw up, have diarrhea, or do something else entirely. Perspiration forms micro drops on his upper lip.

"Good evening, Miss Darla," Tyler responds, slowly bobbing up and down and gripping the newel post until his knuckles whiten. His intestines swell.

"You know what time it is, hon? Friday or not, I know how you younger folks like to stay up at all hours of the night," Darla says to him, leaning on her silver four-pronged cane with tennis balls on the feet. Fat, shiny rings decorate each finger.

Tyler grimaces in an attempt to smile back and act friendly as the contents of his body liquefy and swirl around, threatening to expel all over the fresh grass. He gulps hard, sweat running down his temple now. He checks his watch and then peers up at Darla.

It's only six-thirty, you crotchety old bat!

"Ah, yes, I know, I know..." His stomach burbles. "I'm heading home now."

She grins a mouthful of brown teeth. His stomach makes another noise, one that sends a shock of pressure down his spine, pressing hard on his lower quadrant.

"Actually," he says, "I really need to get up there. I'm not feeling well at all."

A long, thunderous belch bursts from his mouth unbidden and never to be forgotten. His eyes widen, and he presses a clammy hand to his mouth.

The brown smile contorts into a frown of disgust. Darla utters a small cry and turns around to race back to her apartment. Tyler has never seen those little tennis balls move so quickly. He runs up the stairs, feeling so much liquid sloshing around in his torso.

I am never drinking XS again!

He groans as a small fart passes through his attempts at clenching everything shut. Cursing himself, he punches his fist into his pocket in a desperate search for his keys as he rocks back and forth and up and down. Finding the little fob with two single keys, his hands shake. The key scrapes back and forth over the little metal lock. The key couldn't be any tinier, with the lock tinier still as the silver point engraves frantic scratches over the surface.

Connect, damn you!

The key no longer plays with Tyler, sliding firmly into the lock while his hands continue to shake as he turns it. The soothing sound of a metal plug sliding into the door finally makes its appearance.

The door slaps open, and the wall crunches from the inner knob making impact with it. He slams it back shut, activating the deadbolt and lamenting the cost of repairing the hole in the wall. He lets loose another fart, this time loud and wet.

He rushes to the bathroom, trying to unbuckle his tailor-made khakis. The lights flicker on, illuminating the bright-white interior of the bathroom, with white ceramic tile and a marble vanity. His fingers fumble over the buckle as he bobs up and down, desperately trying to hold in liquid feces. Just as the buckle gives and the zipper spreads, he explodes, releasing everything down his leg. Wet slaps hit the floor, splattering and oozing a mudslide over the formerly pristine tile.

His arms go slack, letting the expensive pants clump to the floor and the buckle clanks on the ceramic. Tyler sighs, no longer feeling pressure but enraged with himself. The crumpled pants at his ankles cling to his skin in a sticky brown mess. He curses again, peeling the wet pants from his legs, his white socks tinged brown and green.

"Oh, my Go—" he utters under his breath, holding his nose and retching. He drops the khakis back to the floor, where they settle for the night.

Geez, what if that had happened in Abby's car? Or worse...at the bar?

Tyler blows out a puffy sigh as his stomach lurches again, forcing him to fall onto his knees in front of the toilet. Every muscle in his torso clenches, squeezing each fiber and causing him to heave a cascade of blackness. One flow after the other, the force is so brutal that vomit sprays from his nose. It hits the water at a velocity that causes it to fountain out of the bowl and splatter onto his mirror, the marble countertop, and his ivory hand towels.

This is not normal! His brain screams at the disaster unfolding in front of him. He's desperate to dial 911, but all his muscles are wound tightly, preventing him from moving without lurching again.

Black sick dribbles down the mirror, making small puddles on the counter. The sight triggers his reflex, squeezing again and sending another stream front and back. A pool of sludge collects under his legs. He doesn't care to move and sits there, questioning reality. Tyler's mind goes numb. He's losing volumes of fluid from every orifice.

Why?

He belches again, heaving another wave like a human fire hose. Everything is black now, trading brown and green for dark dissolved organs. His flesh wrings every drop of human moisture, squeezing and heaving. Dark veins creep into the whites of his eyes, and a black mustache drips from his nose. The once-immaculate bathroom is now painted with corruption. Tyler's hands shake on top of the bowl, fingers tapping up and down, in and out.

How am I even alive?

Looking at the mess he made, Tyler wavers, terrified of the landlord's wrath. His weak head bobbles around, a thin trail of black spittle hanging from his lower lip. He shudders to think what the wall behind him looks like. Not wanting to look, he musters a sliver of strength to pop a hand over the toilet paper roll. He flaps his hand downward to remove the first several layers, all covered in sludge, until the fresh white paper shines back at him. He rips a shred off to dab at the black drool.

The bowl is a disaster. He lowers his face over the hole, closing his eyes to avoid retching again. The heat from his insides wafts up to his nose, gracing him with the scent of citrus, herbals, and death. His stomach heaves again, but there's nothing left to give. He finds the strength to quickly push down the plunger and rid himself of the stink.

Once he's able, he puts his dirty hands on the dirty floor, attempting to crawl toward the bedroom, leaving trails in the blackness and smearing it around. As his head continues to bob in surges of strength and weakness, he faintly remembers the airhead.

Her apartment is a little like this, but it's closer to work and has less of an older population. He remembers crawling at her place, too. But why? He never called her by name because he can't honestly remember it. She's the airhead. The raunchy airhead who wears clothes three sizes too small. His muscles are stiff, resisting his urge to stand, so he stays on all fours, trying to remember why he's suddenly thinking about her.

What is her name? Lindsay? Jenni? Kelly?

None of the names ring a bell, but it doesn't matter. He remembers faintly going to a happy hour at a different bar with her and the other sluts from purchasing and materials management. It was raining out, so the night went a little long.

What was that drink?

Tyler taps his fingers in the sludge on the floor, a fog descending over his consciousness, clouding it further as he racks his brain to remember. He slumps back to lean against the vanity, seeing the Jackson Pollock over the back wall for the first time. He sighs, too weak to care. At least his nose has gotten used to the smell, and he's thankful for a calmer gut.

It wasn't Xyloflux... Maybe it wasn't even a drink...

The memory is hidden behind a thin veil—if only he could get a little knife in there to poke a hole in it and see why this memory is now plaguing him. A tickle moves up his spine as he sits slumped against the vanity, and he turns to see her. She has him on his hands and knees, weak and begging. The Rohypnol covers the sides of his vision with black hands. Although weakened, his memory plays at the back of his mind, a fuzzy reminder of his evening with her and the roofies. Even now, his vision tunnels through the darkness.

Did she do it again tonight?

He shakes his head to try to open his vision wider, but the tiny bit of drug that made it into his system before he squirted his insides out punches at the corners of his eyes.

"I'm just going to put this little collar on you, dog," her usually screechy voice came out like evil silk. He felt the leather against his neck and another finger along his spine.

Where were you, Brett? You were my friend!

The tiny sliver of vision he clings to shows him that she's not really there. Not this time.

Thank God for you, Abby. For you and Ben. You saved me from her.

Tyler squints at the wall as the remains of his vision go dark.

Just ten more minutes, please.

He wants to know more before sleep takes him, but the drug won't let him. He slumps over, resting on a bed of his insides and closing his eyes for the night.

Chapter 7

SICK

TIRED EYES FLUTTER OPEN to take in a scene of abstract fluids flung across walls and a countertop. Peeling up from the floor, a man stands on two wobbling appendages to look into a surface that shows another man staring back at him. The man that looks directly back at him is a hollow shell—black circles encompassing sunken bloodshot eyes, with trails of black residue smeared across pale cheeks. He blinks slowly, seeing what appears to be a battered human on the reflective surface, but can't reconcile what it means to be human. He lifts one of the loose appendages hanging from his side and places the lower end over his neck. Seeing the other man copy his move tells him that the human looking back is only himself.

He looks down, seeing black splattered over a white hollow receptacle attached to a dispensing article of some sort. Curious, he reaches down to grip an activating knob. Deep down, he knows he's seen this before. When he turns one of the knobs, clear liquid pours from the dispenser, swirling and mixing with the black sludge in the receptacle. It disappears down a hole in the center, the clear liquid successfully removing the black to reveal a white bowl.

The man sees a series of interesting flappy articles at the end of one long appendage attached near his head. He sticks one of the articles under the running liquid. It feels cool and not harmful—in fact, it removes black filth from the appendage as it did for the receptacle, uncovering pale flesh underneath. He learns. Armed with new knowledge, he sticks the entire series of articles under the fluid, knowing that his safety is no longer of any concern. These flappy articles together, he remembers them as a unit.

That's called a hand, you idiot.

He places the other hand under the running liquid and splashes a volume over the human face on the reflective surface. He turns the activating knob to its starting position, watching the liquid stop. Looking around, he sees a once-pristine white room that has become a slaughter of splattered vomit and excrement.

The cleansing liquid drips slowly off his human chin as his eyes scan the area. He spots two objects on the other side of the room hanging from the wall. He approaches the objects and reaches out to touch them. They are soft, feeling nice under his touch. He notices the cleansing fluid from his fingers absorb into the object. Using the new information, he lifts the soft hanging object to his human face to rub off the remaining cleansing fluid. The man learns faster, taking in his surroundings and making mental notes of everything. After returning to the dispensing unit, he looks back up into the reflective surface. Looking closer, he sees small red marks slashing across his neck in a scaly sort of pattern. He reaches up to touch them. The flesh is smooth, but he feels lumps underneath that follow the pattern of the red webbing.

What are those? Who are you?

He takes another mental note.

The man uses the two wobbling appendages to shuffle into the next area for more information. He looks around at various objects in the room and sees a large, inviting object in the middle of the room. After shuffling next to it, he runs the end of his loose appendage across the surface, finding it soft and pleasant. Using his entire hand, he presses down into it, and it responds by sinking underneath his touch. The man falls on top, allowing the surface to envelop his frame.

No, no, no! Not the bed, you filthy animal! Take a shower!

The mouth lets out a sigh of contentment. Feeling a pain in the head, he decides to stay here, on this soft surface, to close his eyes and stop taking in the sights...to stop learning...for a little while.

***

I shouldn't have brought Metaxysm outside the lab. Even looking at it now, I know something has happened with it. I mean, it used to be quite pretty, cloaking itself when I turned it back and forth. Since the incident at the bar, it looks dull, powdered with oxidation. Maybe I need to think hard about what I put into this thing. Man, I really can't remember everything.

Passion, I know for sure, since Ben gave me a hard time about it. Was it transmission? Trans... trans... transmogrification? Yes, I think that was the one. Wait a minute. Transmogrification? Doesn't that mean change? Oh, no, no, no, that couldn't have been it, could it? I need to double-check this on Monday. Why didn't I write all this down? Next time, I will. I need to get better at being an inventor. Better at beating Tony anyway.

Abby sits at a kitchen chair, not her usual spot of comfort, perhaps subconsciously as a way to punish herself for being careless. She swings her legs back and forth, turning the dulled Metaxysm around, willing for the color to return and the hum to come back and sing to her. If ever there were a time for her to feel inadequate, it is now.

I need to make a new one, or more, on Monday. What if something terrible has happened to Tyler, though? Can Monday wait? Yeah, it can wait—you're just being paranoid. Just text him.

Abby pulls out her phone and scrolls to the line that says, "Tyler Accountant." She knows his last name but never put it in her phone all those years ago, leaving it as just "accountant" to keep from humanizing him.

Abby: Hey, Tyler. Sorry, I got caught up in the lab. I'm on my way now.

Abby: Hey, how are you feeling today? Any better? Do you want me to help you get your car?

When she plops the phone onto the table, it makes a rubbery *thud* from the anti-shock case. She taps her toe on the floor and her fingers on the table. The room's silence bothers her, so she gets up and turns on the single television in her small apartment. She ignores what's on the screen but likes to use it as a white noise maker to drown out her head. It isn't working for her today, but at least the noise makes it sound like someone is there with her to comfort her anxieties.

One of the things she likes to do when feeling alone or bored is read. When diving into someone else's brainchild, she can focus on the author's prose rather than her own. She's prone to cycling through endless what-ifs that drive her crazy, and the solace that reading gives drowns out her head games. Not one single scenario that she has daydreamed about in the past has come true. Her penchant for not letting events play out like they're meant to was the catalyst for her downfall with Lee. She still replays the moments with him in her head, treating each one as a choose-your-own-adventure that could have been her life's cannon had she chosen the "right" ending. It's too bad she hasn't checked out a new library book in over a week and has nothing new to explore.

She swings her leg under her chair, looking down and picking at her nails. They're looking rough and bloody from all the picking. She rubs one of the hardened scales of skin poking out from her cuticle across her bottom lip before sliding it between her teeth to bite it off. Her mind wanders back to Lee again, wondering if she blew it with Tyler, too.

When Lee confessed his feelings to her in college, she didn't know what to say. They'd been best friends since seventh grade, being weird with each other and talking about things that anyone trying to impress a boyfriend or girlfriend wouldn't talk about. He knew gross details about her, and she knew gross details about him. She remembers sitting behind him in math class and poking the inside of his ear with her pencil eraser. When she pulled it out, it was covered in wax. She laughed and showed it to him, telling him how he had ruined her pencil.

Some people would observe them and make "comments." One group of mean girls teased them incessantly about their friendship. One particularly nasty girl even followed them around and sarcastically talked about their future babies and how ugly they would be. She'd sit behind Abby during class and pull strands of her hair out and giggle about just how ugly she thought she was. Lee always supported Abby, helping her forget the bullying with his oddball humor and taste in obscure games and music. Knowing what she knows now, he took solace in her, too.

It was the music, however, that bonded them. They'd spend hours together exploring unknown bands, going to concerts, talking about the music, and learning to play the guitar together. He was much better than Abby at the guitar, and he'd show her tricks her fingers couldn't replicate. Since their falling out, she hasn't been able to pick up her guitar in the same way or hear the bands they talked about for countless hours in the same way either. She has created a new world for herself since he walked out of the old one, and this new one is full of strangers.

How things ended with Lee formed a relationship scar that affected how Abby relates to others. She has tried to change, but the walls she builds are strong, and as delightful others, except Tony, find her to be, her interactions are an act.

She picks up her phone after her long daydream of Lee. Tyler still hasn't replied. She puts the phone face down on the table and sighs, staring at it for a moment.

I'll just take a nap and sleep it away.

She routinely uses sleep as an escape, hoping her dreams will reveal life's secrets to her and pass the time until her next anxiety session. She backs the chair out from the table, scraping it against the cheap linoleum, and stands. Staring at the phone again, willing Tyler to text her back, she sighs again and drifts to the couch to lie down. The television's ambient noise fades into black as she closes her eyes and shuts off her mind.

***

After some time passes, the man opens his eyes. The room is a little darker but still light. Driven by instinct, he gets back up on wobbly lower appendages and moves toward the white room with the white bowl. He remembers seeing a larger receptacle, square shaped, in the corner of the same room with a larger dispensing unit. If the larger dispensing unit leaks clear liquid like the small one, the man can use it to clean off the human body too.

That's called a shower, and you need it, you disgusting pig.

He slinks toward the square receptacle, glaring at the tiny reflective surface that covers the dispensing unit. A distorted yellow copy glares back when the hand creeps over the handle and fumbles with it. It is different than the smaller one, but he learns fast. A spray of clear cleansing liquid flows from above him, hitting the opposite side of the wall before running down to the floor hole, where the fluid swirls out of sight.

The man looks down, remembering that a bright-colored second skin above the lower appendages has covered him the whole time. Seeing a row of shiny studs running up the front of this strange cover, the man uses the agility afforded to him by the little hands to unfasten them. He lets the cover drop to the floor, then uses his lower appendage to kick it aside. He's getting more robust and better about using this new body.

He strides into the receptacle, feeling the cold cleansing liquid flow over the head and down over the rest of the human form. The feeling of instinct kicks in again, drawing his eyes toward the oblong shape sitting in a tray. He picks it up and moves it around, creating soft bubbles. He runs the oblong shape all over his body, watching as the bubbles carry dark liquid down his appendages and over bony flippers at the end of his wobbly attachments.

Hands, fingers, feet, toes, arms, legs. What is wrong with you?

He remembers now—these are the names of the human parts.

He turns what he now remembers to be soap around and around again in his hand, watching the bubbles condense into thick foam. He puts the soap down and uses both hands to scrub his face. The liquid is so refreshing and cold over his hot skin. He dares to open the hole in his head to take some of the liquid in. The sensation travels throughout his form, renewing him. He curls the hole in his face upward into a grin, relishing in the relief the fluid offers him. He opens his eyes again to look down at his human body.

Something seems different but welcome. He feels a tiny budding protrusion from behind him, above the legs, and on the flat surface under the neck. It is only about the size of his smallest hand finger. He flicks it with the longest finger and feels the shock of light pain at the impact.

Argh, stop that! What is that?

He learns more. A new mobility unit? Delicately, he squeezes it with the fingers to feel that it is soft. It releases a clear, sticky substance that feels slippery as it rinses under the cleansing fluid. The man uses the fingers to test the new substance. He brings the fingers to the nose to see if he can smell it—no smell, just sticky.

Gross, stop! What is going on?

He looks around to see if there are more of these new units. To the man's surprise, there are a few more. Not many, just a few. He tests the new protrusions to see more of the same sticky substance releasing from them. They're the same little things with the same sticky stuff—maybe some fresh legs are growing. The man begins to feel exhilarated. Soon, he will have more legs to help move his body, and he can use the arms and hands to concentrate on other things. After finishing the refreshing cleansing ritual, he returns to the reflective surface. The eyes are still bloodshot, with black centers and a hazy covering over them. He looks around the room at the black splattered mess that never left. Now that the body has been cleansed, the man decides not to spend too much time in this room. It is dirty.

Go back in there and clean up. What do you think you're doing?

With a mild wobble on the two legs, the man moves to the room with the soft platform and sits, sinking low and feeling relaxed.

As he sits, a strange taste fills his mouth. It is rich and full of flavor and also fills his nose. A rush of excitement shivers over the pale flesh, causing the fingers to twitch and the new sticky leg sprouts behind him to grow slightly longer and wider. There's another reflective surface nearby, and he can see that the extra parts that only a moment ago were the size of a tiny finger now look like one of his arms.

What just happened? What is that taste in my mouth, blood?

The sudden growth spurt of the appendages has drained some energy. The man becomes sleepy once again and lies across the bed to close the eyes.

He begins to dream a most pleasant dream. He strides along a dark, twisted path, the strange sounds of crackling earth and fear surrounding him. He smiles wide, showing rows of little white squares known as teeth. The exciting aroma fills his nose and mouth, affirming his path and pushing him forward. Inside, however, his head screams in protest.

***

Abby opens her eyes. She didn't dream this time, depriving her of much-needed escapism. The TV is loud as she comes out of the dead of sleep. It plays an old sitcom she never watched when she was younger but finds herself drawn to now, hoping the canned laughter will pull her out of her head. After turning the volume down to suit her post-nap ears, she turns her phone over and over in her palm, the screen face still black with no return text from Tyler. She rubs her eyes and yawns when her brain starts talking to her again.

Maybe I need to call Ben. Or maybe Byron? No, I shouldn't call Byron—I don't know what would happen if he knew I'd taken Metaxysm out of the lab. Ben didn't seem to know what any of these things meant, though. If I text Tyler again, will he think I'm desperate? No, that can't be true—the guy nearly threw up in my car. Or other things. Maybe he's embarrassed. I told him not to poop in my car. I have to let him know it's okay and I'm not upset with him.

Abby: Hey, Tyler. Sorry, I got caught up in the lab. I'm on my way now.

Abby: Hey, how are you feeling today? Any better? Do you want me to help you get your car?

Abby: Hey, Tyler. Are you okay?

That's the only thing she can think of to say to him. It expresses her concern without sounding desperate, or like she's trying anything with him. Tyler's unanswered texts and her wild thoughts creep into anxiety, so she decides to call her mom. The phone rings until the call is just about to click over to voicemail, and then her mother's voice comes through.

"Well, hello, Abigail. What are you up to these days?"

Abby's relationship with her parents is different. Typically, long stretches of time elapse between phone calls or texts. It's not because Abby doesn't love her parents or that they don't love her; it's usually because Abby loses track of time so quickly that one day turns into a week, and then before she knows it, a month goes by. Her mom isn't good about calling her either, and her dad isn't good with cell phones.

"Oh, not much today. I think I messed something up. though."

"Messed something up? At work?"

Every time they talk, her parents tell her how impressed they are with her career and achievements. Their declarations continue to surprise her, as she always calls her mom when things go wrong. In the past, she has called to complain about her problems with Tony and all of her failed gadgets. Even as a biologist, she'd complain about feeling like a waste of resources, time, and energy for the company.

"Yes, I think I messed something up big time."

"How so?"

"I, uh, may have brought one of my gadgets out of the lab last night."

She can hear her mom *tsk* on the other side.

"You know you're not supposed to do that, Abs."

"I know, I know…" She shakes her head, knowing her mom can't see her. "But I really thought it was broken. My computer didn't activate it right."

"What happened then?"

Abby tells her about going to Chrysalis Lounge and running into Tyler. She colors the story in an accusatory voice against him and shares how he drunkenly grabbed the device from her and dropped it into his drink.

"I mean, that was *his* fault, right? I didn't tell him to do that!"

"You're right, he shouldn't have done that. So what is the mess-up?"

"I don't really know if it was a mess-up—I just *think* I messed up. He seemed really sick last night and hasn't returned my texts."

"Oh, honey, he's a guy. He's probably not paying attention to his phone, or he's not interested in you. I wouldn't worry about it too much."

"Ouch, Mom."

"Well, it's true! Just ask your father."

"You weren't there, though. I don't know how to explain it, but I'm pretty sure that if he's seen my text, he'd be responding to it."

As she speaks with her mom, she thinks about her next action plan. It takes over her mind to where she can no longer concentrate on having a constructive conversation with her mother. Rather than wait until Monday, she will see if Tyler picked up his car, and then she will make up for her mistake by creating another Metaxysm tomorrow.

"I'll let you know what I find out," she tells her mom, "but I have to go now."

"Okay, well, I love you. Be careful!"

Abby says goodbye and looks out the window. The sun is creeping down the horizon.

I'll go to Soto first thing tomorrow morning.

***

The man awakes again, pleased with the visions that appeared behind his eyes. With renewed energy, the body sits upright with the help of the mobility units. Rechecking the reflective surface, he sees the new appendages have fully grown and have extended beyond the human legs to coil beneath the soft platform onto the floor. The man counts six new legs. Feeling a new wave of excitement, he sees tiny black orbs attached underneath the new legs.

He pokes one with the human finger, and it wiggles free. It lands on the soft platform, wriggling around and unfurling its own mobility units. The man smiles at the little thing as it scurries away and out of the room. Several more black orbs drop and scurry away after their brother. The man's insides feel strange. There is a heat, a special warmth, that causes one of the moving parts inside of him to pump faster. He swells with joy.

What...the...hell...is...that?

It's time to move; the visions say so. The man looks out the clear cutout in the wall to see that darkness has spread. He opens his mouth and sucks in a breath, feeling and tasting the bloody residue on his tongue. It tells him things. It tells him to leave now.

He slithers through the bedroom into the hall, passing the open maw of the guest bedroom where a nest has developed in the center while he slept. Inside the nest is a writhing mess of black bubbles, each pulling up every once in a while to open a mouth and chirp like baby birds waiting for their meal. The man blushes again, a thick yellow pallor spreading where pink would generally show. The organ inside beats faster, and he places the human hands over the chest. The appendages sway, bumping into walls and doors, coating them with fluid.

The landlord is going to kill me.

He has no time to waste. He gives a final longing look at the black nest before slithering into the main area, coating his path with more of the slime. He uses the fingers to turn the round, shiny object, which opens a gateway to the outer world.

The man is cautious, using only the human feet to creep through corridors and stairwells of the strange new world. Precious lubrication is to be reserved for fast travel from now on. One area in the corridor has a peculiar object on the floor. It's curvy, with little green sticks poking out of it. The man attempts to avoid the object, but one of the appendages accidentally knocks it over, making a loud crash.

You just knocked over Mrs. Dunst's spider plant, you dolt! She's going to be so pissed at you!

After the crashing noise, there's a slamming noise from down below. The man mustn't be seen until he meets his mate. He tiptoes down the stairs, then peers around the corner but sees nothing. There must have been something, but nothing is there now.

Someone heard you.

Now out of sight, he uses his touch memory to feel his way around the darkness. Halos of light are equally placed along this hard path. With fast travel, he avoids the lights, ducking into the pines and toward the dark path in his dreams.

Chapter 8

Trek

IT'S THE MIDDLE OF the night. Where are you going?

The calm night air is warm and humid. Night chirps winnow through the air as nocturnal insects call for their mates. Leaves rustle, and the scent of pine rises with the heat.

Stop walking, turn around! Why do my feet hurt so bad?

Tyler looks down to see the cracked and bleeding toenails threatening to crumble away. His human instinct is to turn around and rest away the Xyloflux from the night before, but invisible strings drag him along as he marionettes through the woods.

I think I'm going to lose my toenails. Damn, my head hurts.

He tries to put a hand to his brow, but his veins are filled with lead, and only the impulse is permitted to move.

What the...

Blisters swell out from the pads of his feet, sending pangs of fire through his flesh. The puppet master lifts a leg and dunks one foot into a mud puddle, followed by the other, creating a dirt shell around his feet that only mildly alleviates the pain.

I'm going to have a nasty infection tomorrow. Why won't you stop walking?

Tyler is overwhelmed with exhaustion. He tries to close his eyes, but the thing won't let him. All he can do is haze his vision, hoping that whatever is happening is only a dream and he will wake from this nightmare in a clean room with a clean bathroom. As he wills his eyes to unfocus, wisps of vile thoughts unfurl icy tendrils on his mind.

I better not lose control right now.

Putting selfish needs behind him, Tyler internally reboots to stay alert. The encroaching thoughts grip for purchase on the sides of his brain, but they lose the battle and slink back to the pit they came from.

I am still me, but I am a monster. What happened? Was it the roofies mixed with XS? It can't be... surely some sicko has done that before.

The air twinkles with yellow spots that pulse in random patterns, reminding Tyler of his childhood days catching fireflies at twilight with his sister and cousins. He watches them blink, remembering his cousin, Alice, proudly holding a glass jar full of the winking bugs and declaring names for all of them.

The impulse continues to lull him forward, making a new pair of mud shoes.

The wet *plunk* into the mud hole stirs another memory of teaching his sister, Naomi, how to skip rocks across the lake at their house in the Ozarks. She could never do it right, picking large, chunky rocks rather than the smooth disc-shaped pebbles needed to frisbee the thing across the surface.

Plunk plunk.

Tyler's heart is sick. His feet are unstoppable, and he would never have imagined during those days long ago while catching lighting bugs or skipping rocks with his family that his life would end here, in these woods, by this master. There is still so much he would like to do and experiences he would like to have.

I wish I had been able to call my parents one last time to tell them I love them.

As the strings guide him forward, his peripheral vision catches sight of the ghastly appendages swaying around him. They hover in the air, appearing gentle and harmless. Tyler knows the truth— the truth that claws at him every moment— these tentacles mean to kill.

His heart thumps in his chest. In the distance, two men lounge near a ratty tent, one lying in the grass and the other sitting upright, looking around. His heart pumps faster, and an evil urge rises up his neck to fill his vision with a red halo of rage.

No, leave them alone. Leave them alone! Just stop walking already!

As he moves closer, his vision is infringed by the redness, creating only a pinprick of color to highlight the men. A rattling sound hums and Tyler feels his neck vibrate in sync with the noise. He tries again to use his hands to feel around his head and neck, but again, the master thwarts his attempts.

They aren't hurting anyone. Just walk on by.

Grass tickles his feet as he continues to march forward, intent on elimination.

Just walk by.

Closer and closer, the sitting man looks up at Tyler. His eyes are wide and wet, mouth agape. Tyler sees the blood coursing through the man in a network of capillaries spider-webbed throughout his body. It pumps harder and faster the closer he approaches.

How am I seeing this?

He locks eyes with the man. A middle-aged, scrawny pile of bones locks eyes in return. His face is covered in patchy fuzz, with the pumping capillaries peeking from between spots. The icy, vile thoughts intrude again, planting suggestions of destruction in his mind. The tentacles sway in response, waiting for instruction as the internal tug tells him to destroy.

Stop! Leave him alone! Stop it, stop it, stop!!

Tyler wrestles his brain, imagining slamming the gray matter into the front of his skull to force himself forward and ignore the urge. He tastes the tang of blood in his mouth and thinks of Abby. A thought occurs to him to reason with the master.

You don't want these men. They don't mean anything to you.

The flavor intensifies, filling his head with more thoughts of Abby. She smiles at him in his mind's eye— her gray eyes shimmer in the sunlight with a halo of wavy frizz encircling her crown. He wants to find her and take her home to be with him and stay with him.

The man in the grass trembles and curls his body backward, away from Tyler, as he continues to stare.

He means nothing to you.

His heart beats so hard that his mind is clouded with the rhythmic *thump-thump-thumps* ringing in his ears. The taste of blood quivers in his mouth in a crescendo, blacking out the vision of the man in the grass to make way for the woman who waits for him.

The strings pull him forward again, passing through their camp and disappearing into the fold of trees.

Oh, thank God...

Tyler isn't sure whether his will turned the beast within or if it was the sudden thoughts of Abby that made it change its mind.

What if Abby is in trouble now?

Something has shifted in Tyler. He realizes that whatever thought or feeling caused her to crop up in his mind could be shared with the beast.

She could be its target now... I have to stay focused. He is probably dragging me to her place.

Tyler watches the scenery blur by while powerless to stop it. Owls hoot, and raccoons chitter as he passes, finding refuge in the shadow of the foliage and away from the horror. Time passes as he acts like a paralyzed passenger on this journey while the sun peaks overhead, threatening them with visibility and heat. The morning heat proves formidable, instantly causing discomfort and more boils to swell. The warm heaviness weakens Tyler, and he fears that if he gives in, he will lose everything— even any slight control he might have had would be gone.

He tries to remember his parents.

His dad was so proud that day he earned his CPA, lauding that he was the first member of the family to go through college. Tyler's efforts encouraged his sister, who ended up becoming a nurse at Memorial Mercy West.

His mother has been such a pillar of strength in his life.

I wonder if I'll ever see them again.

The heat is unbearable, and his vision starts to blacken the way it did the night after happy hour. He knows he's losing it.

Tyler's consciousness wanes as his exhausted brain craves the comfort of a soft bed. His body continues to carry him forward on invisible strings while his mind is only along for the ride. The fight in him fades.

Please, just let me rest, lie down and sleep...

Wait, why am I at Soto?

Chapter 9

DEDICATION

SHADOWS CAST VERTICAL ORANGE stripes across the wall while Abby lounges in her overstuffed princess settee. She plays on her phone while soft indie music swims through her headset, drowning out the world's sounds—her phone pings, alerting her to a new text.

Ben: What are you doing right now?

Abby: Just sitting around. Why? What's up?

Ben: Can I come by? I'm bored.

Abby: Sure. Do you know how to get here?

Ben: Yep. Be there soon.

Making a face, she hurries to get out of her sweatpants and into something more presentable. As she pauses before choosing a shirt, a thought itches her brain that maybe Ben is going to be Lee all over again. She opts for the hoodie that swallows her body like a mouse in a box. Looking hard in the mirror, she musses up her hair.

Ben is harmless.

There is a sharp rap at the door.

That was quick...

Trotting to the door, she knows Ben lives at least fifteen minutes away. Surely this couldn't be him because he's never been to her house.

The moment she opens the door a crack, Ben barges inside.

"Whoa, hey!" Abby stumbles backward, nearly falling over.

"What's up?" He strolls to her sofa and plops down on it, putting his feet on the coffee table.

Abby peers at him. "I'm glad you're comfortable, but could you please take off your shoes?"

"Oh, sorry!" He slips his shoes off and tosses them near the front of the door next to Abby. A chunk of dried mud breaks off the sole and shatters on her entry tile.

She stares at the dirt clod and looks back up at Ben. *When did he get the beer?*

"Nice place," he says, looking around and sipping from the can.

"Thanks?" Abby's confusion rides right over his head.

"So what do you want to do?" he asks.

"I don't know. You were the one who was bored. What do you want to do?"

Ben takes his feet off the table and plants them on the floor. He slides the beer can across the table, leaving a wet trail. Abby doesn't like the way he's looking at her.

"You know what I want to do."

"Um, listen to music?" She tries to avoid his gaze.

"Nope."

He gets up from the couch and starts walking toward her.

"Play video games?" Sweat forms on Abby's upper lip.

"Nope."

He's now standing inches from her.

"Uh, go for a r-ride?" She turns her head from his hot, hop-laced breath.

"Nope." His word sends a puff of air at her face, blowing a strip of hair back and filling her nostrils.

"We work together," she says, her shoulders trembling.

"I don't care who sees us," he says. He reaches out and lightly touches her hand with a finger.

"I'm going to put in some music." She withdraws her hand and presses it to the back of her sweatpants. She grabs the first album sitting on the shelf and slides it into the deck.

"Retro, I like that," Ben remarks.

The music swells, playing The Police's "Every Little Thing She Does is Magic."

Wait, not that one. Abby raises a finger to switch to the next song when she feels Ben's hand gripping hers and pushing it down.

"I like this song," he says.

"Well, I don't."

"Leave it."

Her heart pounds at his hand on hers. He turns her around. The tip of his nose is touching hers.

"Stop it, Ben," she says, tears beginning to burn in her eyes.

"Nope."

He grabs her and pulls her close.

"Get off me, Ben, I'm warning you. I'll complain to Jon."

He doesn't let go.

"Get off me!"

Her threats go unnoticed as he squeezes her tighter.

"Stop it, stop it!" she screams.

She tries to push him away, using her arms and legs to pry him off. Her hands find a way to grip his shoulders, and she pushes hard, feeling the pressure give and a crack ring out. She dislocates both of his shoulders.

Ben screams in pain as he throws his neck back. Abby hears a sickening snap as his neck breaks. Her heart pounds as she drops him to the floor, the music from the album playing a grotesque soundtrack to the horror unfolding in front of her. His body flops lifeless to the floor as his head rolls to the side, revealing bloodshot eyes and a small line of blood trickling from an open mouth.

"Oh, my God, what have I done?"

Abby jumps up and runs toward the mirror to look at herself. What she sees reflecting back is unrecognizable. Large black irises are set into bloody whites, with dark circles and black sludge smeared all over her face. She reaches up to touch it, screaming soundlessly into a void. A pit in her stomach grows—a feeling of intensified lack of control of her body. She feels possessed.

As she looks back at Ben's body crumpled in a heap on the floor, his hair is different. His face is different. His skin bubbles and boils, popping puddles of pus on her laminate floor. His face sloughs away and spatters to the floor, leaving behind a new face. A familiar face. Lee.

***

Abby shoots upright with hair matted to the side of her face. Still sitting in bed, she feels the lingering energy pulse in her gut from the dream. The Sunday sun rises, piercing its warm rays through a slit in the blackout curtains. Still shaking, she rubs a sleep-crusted eye while picking up her phone to check for any midnight return messages from Tyler. None. She yawns, runs a hand over her face, and then pulls her hair back.

What was that supposed to mean?

Thoughts of Tyler tickle her mind. Her feelings wax and wane as she thinks about him. The idea of her dud of an invention possibly hurting someone pains her. She tries to text him again.

> Abby: Hey, Tyler. Sorry, I got caught up in the lab. I'm on my way now.

> Abby: Hey, how are you feeling today? Any better? Do you want me to help you get your car?

> Abby: Hey, Tyler. Are you okay?

> Abby: Hey, are you okay?

She tosses her phone onto the nightstand to wait for his reply while she gets ready. Her shower thoughts spin around the four attributes and what they possibly could have done to him. Her wildest imagination sends pangs of anxiety through her chest, hoping her gadget is indeed a dud and Tyler is using the weekend to sleep off the XS. She waits an hour before giving in to the fact that he's not texting her back. *Maybe Mom is right, and he is not interested in me anymore?*

She sits on the edge of her bed, tapping her toes on the floor. Then she swipes her keys and heads to work.

***

The journey to Soto Labs is short. Rather than go straight to the building right away, Abby pulls into the parking lot of Chrysalis Lounge. There it is—Tyler's coupe still parked in the spot like a cherry-red beacon. The two cars that had squeezed him in on Friday were gone, abandoning his vehicle as a lone sentry to the bar's empty lot. Abby sighs and taps her index finger on the wheel.

Don't worry. He's fine.

She pulls away from Chrysalis to head toward Soto.

Abby has never tried to badge into the building on a weekend, so she isn't sure it will work. As she pulls up the winding path to the well-hidden building's clearing, she sees the late-morning sun as it glows over the surface of the nondescript black reflective glass. The empty parking lot temporarily makes Abby mourn the lack of company. Regardless, she trudges forward, scanning her badge and going inside, engulfed by the cold lab.

The echo of silence in the atrium is formidable, almost deafening. Abby makes her way to B6, traveling through the worm and into the main lab area. She didn't bring lunch today, knowing her mission is to get in and get out. She badges in to see that her lab has remained untouched since Friday.

"Go-o-od mor-ning, Ab-i-gail P-p-prin-ce." Frankie boots on and drags through its sequence.

While waiting for the computer, Abby hastens to the lab and takes down several little blue panels. She moves quickly, hammering each delicate piece, and folds over and over to make her metal cube pastry. The lab echoes with the song of the hammered metal as she begins to make a second Metaxysm.

Hammer, fold, hammer, fold, repeat, and repeat until the second cube is complete. The song fills her with determination to appease the growing anxiety monster in her stomach.

"S-s-s-yst-em wa-a-rning." The familiar completion of the boot sequence rings out from the office.

Abby tends to the computer corpse and opens the Animate program. The seedling progress bar begins its initiation. She wastes no time, moving back toward the lab while Animate loads.

Hammer, fold, hammer, fold...number three.

She repeats her method of hammering and folding the singing blue metal into pastry squares until she's accumulated seven of them.

She then lines them up on the counter and places a single watch glass in front of each. She grabs the first box of Metamorphosis and places it on the counter. There are several backup kits of the same item. She grabs the biological Paroxysm kit and puts it next to Metamorphosis. She has seven biological kits left, the limiting factor to her attempts at saving Tyler.

After opening the lab drawers, she collects precisely seven of the Erlenmeyer flasks she had used before. She mixes all the components using one flask at a time, seeing the familiar green liquid spin around on the stir plate. Abby is determined to get at least one functioning Metaxysm without waiting until Monday to use Ben's computer; she's creating an insurance plan by creating several. Surely Frankie can get at least *one* out of seven right.

Even though she didn't take notes, the rush of fear forces the memory of her order of addition, and she follows in her footsteps exactly. She cannot risk making any changes. The original Metaxysm may have held the key to reversing the effects, but she will never know since it has been used up already with two corrupted files.

She reasons that making a working Metaxysm may at least help heal Tyler's abdominal distress.

She moves through the routine of letting the metal pastry soak up the fluid and bake in the low-temperature oven. One after the other, Abby pulls out each successive turquoise cube from the oven until her replication task is complete.

Making the cubes is the easy part; connecting the cubes to Frankie will be the challenge. She places the first cube onto the activation pad, sets the parameters, and hits "activate." Rather than walk away, this time, she chooses to watch. The first attempt is a colossal failure. After a few minutes, the computer lets loose a loud beep and spits out a premature data log: *Passion...corrupt data...corrupt data...c orrupt data.*

The only characteristic this cube gets is Passion—the one thing Ben had a fit over during happy hour.

Abby sighs loudly, plunking the cube into a reject pile and picking up the next one.

Following the same protocol, she begins to activate the new cube.

Another loud beep and premature log.

Excitement...Passion...corrupt...corrupt...corrupt...corrupt.

"Dang," she mutters through gritted teeth, picking up the failed cube and tossing it aside in exchange for a new one.

Activation begins on the new cube—another loud beep. Abby kicks the wall.

Transmogrification...Rebirth...Melody...corrupt...corrupt...corrupt.

Abby perks up at the new characteristic. Melody? She puts the new cube aside at the start of a "maybe" pile. She places a sticky note in front of it, scrawled with the three characteristics from the program.

She places the fourth cube on the activation pad.

Excitement...Melody...Transmogrification...Rebirth...corrupt...corrup t.

With the new Melody feature, she places this cube with the previous one in the "maybe" pile. Three more cubes remain, waiting to fail.

Passion...Melody...Excitement...corrupt...corrupt...corrupt.

Abby sucks in a breath through her closed teeth. She has accepted that she won't get anything more than four attributes at most. It comes down to the combination of attributes that she'll have to determine its function. She grips the final cube in her fist, saying a gentle prayer over it, hoping for a set of attributes that could potentially help Tyler. With shaking fingers, she positions the final cube on the activation pad.

"Please..." she says to Frankie as she hits the "activate" button.

She's motionless, staring intently at the computer as the progress bar mocks her.

Excitement...Passion...Transmogrification...Rebirth...Melody...Rectification.

A long, heavy breath whooshes from her lips—one she didn't realize she was holding.

"Are you kidding me? And one to spare!" she rejoices to all her broken lab parts while tucking the unactivated cube neatly in a top drawer. Picking up the cube, she looks deeply into it. Turning it sideways makes it almost disappear like before, yet a calm, soft glow emanates from the center.

Melody, Melody, Melody... What does that mean? Rectification? Maybe that's the key...

The air is silent as she observes her object.

Bang, bang, bang!

A rhythmic knock pounds on her lab door and echoes across the walls. She almost drops her perfect activation, squeezing it tightly in her fist as she whips her head over to see Byron's face at her window. Relieved, she moves to the door. She cracks it open and peers through at him.

"What are you doing here?" she asks.

"I'm always here on Sunday."

"Does Jon know you come in on Sundays?"

"Yep."

"Why do you do it?"

"Because I need to create. What are *you* doing here on Sunday?" He pokes a fat finger at her.

Abby looks down at the secret in her closed fist. "I had to make something right."

"Let me in."

Byron pushes gently through the door, and Abby complies with his bulk. She stumbles back as he looks around.

"Hmm, pristine," he remarks. "I like it." He peeks over at the disheveled office beyond the lab benches. "Not so pristine."

"Are you here actually making something? Since you barged into *my* lab, can I see what *you're* doing?"

Byron shrugs. "Sure. Come on." He turns to leave the lab, and Abby follows, still clutching Metaxysm 2.0 in an iron grip.

Moving out of her lab, they wander to Byron's lab, where he scans his badge and opens the door for her. As she moves inside, she takes in the scene. Byron's lab isn't nearly as neatly organized as hers. Panels are scattered across the countertops and empty kit boxes overflow from the trash can. Broken ampules lie on the counter, forming a dried crusty residue over the surface from leaking fluids. Byron has both white and ivory kits as well. There's a strange acrid aroma in the air, mingled with maple over the undercurrent of Byron's body odor. Abby senses he must spend quite a bit of time in here.

The hooks that typically hold the metal panels on the far end of Byron's lab are practically empty, although a few scant red and black ones are still clinging to their hooks, waiting to be used. Various created objects litter the countertops and floors. Craning her neck to see the office, she sees more objects taking up space.

"Wow," she says as Byron closes the door and steps past her. "What do all these things do?"

Byron says nothing.

She eyeballs a large object on the counter—a black sphere-shaped container about two feet in diameter. There's a single viewport on the side, right above the seam where the top and bottom connect.

"What is that?" she asks, pointing at the object.

Byron moves toward it and presses the lid. Its magnetized clasp gives, and the sphere opens, releasing a hermetically sealed hiss. The inside is empty, the lights from his office reflecting on a smooth inner surface.

"Nothing yet," he says after a while.

Abby relaxes and smiles, impressed at the craftsmanship.

"You have a lot going on in here," she says.

"Mmm." He nods.

"How come we haven't heard of any of your inventions making it out? I mean, surely something got a patent with all the things you have in here? Right?"

"Nah. Tony always steals my stuff."

Byron's response takes Abby by surprise. He says the thing as if it were common knowledge and not something worth fighting.

Open-mouthed, she stares at him. "What the hell, Byron? How does this happen? And why does it seem like you don't even care?"

Byron shrugs again. "I have some things he doesn't know about."

"So you're telling me what he showed us on Friday was yours?"

"Actually...no. But it was a really good invention of Ben's."

Abby shakes her head again, eyes wide. "You mean, it's true? He really stole the idea from Ben? And you *knew*?"

"Yeah, he's a slippery one."

Abby sighs. "I don't understand why you'd let that happen."

"What do you have in your hand?" Byron points toward Abby's closed fist, which holds the fully activated cube. His abrupt change in topic nearly knocks her over. Her hand jolts to her chest, and she squeezes the cube tighter.

"It-it's what I was working on when you scared the crap out of me earlier."

"Show me."

Abby eyes him. She'd never known him to be so open and demanding. She tentatively unfurls her fingers, the little cube resting in her hand. Its sharp angles dug into her skin, leaving dents where she clasped the object tightly. Byron plucks it from her palm.

"B-be so incredibly careful with that," she says. Her heart leaps in her chest, and she reaches out, knowing she won't be able to re-create this if Byron's big sausage fingers crush it.

He turns it back and forth, seeing how it disappears and reappears based on how the light hits it. He grunts and cracks a small smile. "Neat. What does it do?"

"I'm not sure yet. I'd just activated it when you came by."

"Well, what are its attributes then?"

Abby closes her eyes to remember.

"Uh...Excitement, Passion, Transmogrification, Rebirth, Melody, and Rectification. I've made it before, but my crap computer corrupted some files, so I had to repeat it six more times to get it right. Please don't drop it."

He laughs in a deep baritone. "This sounds crazy dangerous."

"Wha...? Dangerous? How?" Her stomach clenches as her mind goes back to Tyler.

"Yeah, totally dangerous if you use it the wrong way."

"Um, can you please enlighten me?"

Byron turns the cube around in his fat fingers. His gaze is pensive as he strokes his scruffy chin with his other hand. "Well, usually the last two attributes are the reverse of the first four." He rubs his chin again. "I suppose the most concerning point would be Transmogrification. Probably Rebirth, too, depending on the Transmog."

"Byron, I'm really confused. Can you please help me out?"

"With these things, it's always a crap shoot. The first four attributes can occur in any order. The last two are specific." He hands it back to her, and she clutches it tightly again.

"So what do you mean by the last two are the reverse? Or specific? I have Melody, then Rectification. What does that mean?"

"It means that when you either sing to it or play music for it, then the last thing will happen in that order."

"How do you know that?"

"It's not hard to figure out."

"Says you! No one ever taught me these things!"

"No one taught me either. I just figured things out. Plus, I've been here a while."

Abby is incredulous. Her previous prejudice against Byron being slow and thoughtless has just been squashed.

"Byron, I have to tell you something."

He looks up at her with deep-set wrinkles around his eyes. "Mmm?"

"I may have had an accident with a previous version of this object."

His eyes bore into her. It makes her uncomfortable, so she shifts from one foot to bear weight on the other.

"Go on..."

"This is my seventh attempt at making this invention. I may have inadvertently tested it the first time."

"Explain."

Abby tells Byron about the corrupted files on Metaxysm 1.0 and how she got some of her blood on it after it was activated. She shares how she brought it to happy hour, and Tyler dropped it into his glass just before he drank some XS. She finishes by explaining how he became suddenly ill, stunk up her car, and didn't respond to her texts.

"I hope I didn't make him sick," she says with a grimace and a shrug.

Byron stares at her. Either he has gone to la-la land during her explanation, or the wheels are grinding so hard in his head that the muscles of his face have stopped working. After a moment, Abby gives him a "well?" shrug.

He opens his mouth and pauses before speaking. "I have bad news. But I also have some good news."

"Okay, please break the bad news to me first."

"Your invention has most likely infected Tyler. If they haven't already, the first four attributes will show themselves any time now. The two corrupted files may have caused a corrupted outcome, but it's hard to tell. It may be that the last two attributes never existed in the first version.

"Is-is that *all*?"

"Yes. The good news is if you can use the same reagents and method to create multiple copies, there won't be much variability in the outcome. So most likely, if you made this the same way you did before, it's the same object, just more complete with the uncorrupted pieces."

Abby bites her lip. She doesn't like the word *infected*. It sounds like a patient-zero situation rather than just a run-of-the-mill stomach bug. Plus, she was a little fond of Tyler before he became a belligerent drunk and farted in her car.

"So if I sing to it or play music, the last thing happens, right?"

"Yep."

"And the last thing is Rectification, which means 'fix,' right? So if I sing to it now, will it fix Tyler?"

"Not in here." Byron waves a finger around the room, making an implication about the steel housings surrounding the underground. "But you can test it."

"Without wasting it, I hope?"

"It won't be wasted if it was properly activated."

Abby looks at the cube in her palm. It's such a beautiful little thing. Something this beautiful couldn't possibly be capable of causing any harm. She clears her throat and begins to hum softly.

There are no words to her ballad, just instrumental humming. The cube begins to respond all the same. As she hums, it glows a little brighter. It initiates itself and levitates from her palm, just inches above. Her eyes widen, and her song threatens to break, but she catches herself and continues after only a slight warble in her voice. Byron leans against the lab counter, picking at his nails and occasionally looking up at the glowing blue cube.

The cube spins faster and faster as her song continues. The layers pulse as it turns, disappearing and reappearing in a strobe-like effect. Small blue beams of light emit from the center, spinning and searching around the room like a disco ball. Byron continues to lean against the counter, watching the lights. The lights wander as if lost, trying to search for a target as they flit around the room. The cube halts its spin, and the blue beams eject a final energy pulse with a deep thrum.

Metaxysm drops back into Abby's palm with a soft *putt*, quiet as it once was. The cube remains a turquoise color, ready to be activated again.

"All right, that was pretty neat," she tells Byron, who has turned around and started working on something else.

"Byron, I feel so stupid. All the time, I feel dumb." She turns Metaxysm 2.0 back and forth in her fingers.

"Why? You're here just like everyone else."

"I just don't know what any of this means. This is my first time making a successful object, and I don't know why it works the way it does. I also don't know why my computer fails to activate them."

"Tony put your computer together before you got here. He doesn't like you."

Abby jerks her wide eyes to Byron. "*Tony* put Frankie together?" Her stomach flops. Her mild adoration for the quirky instrument melts into disdain.

"Yep."

"Byron! Would Tony try to sabotage me?"

Byron turns to her and peers above a tiny set of spectacles she didn't realize he had put on while his back was to her. "Ah, hm. Yep."

Abby stamps her foot and pounds the bench with a fist. "Why does this go unpunished? Why is he allowed to do this?" she screeches through a tightened larynx, making her cough.

Byron shrugs and bobs his head back and forth. "What can we do about it? He's the CEO's son."

Abby wants to faint. The influx of information Byron keeps loading on her without a care is overwhelming. She steadies herself on the bench.

"Giving people the benefit of the doubt isn't a bad thing, though," Byron says.

"I wonder if any of my other gadgets would have worked correctly if I'd attached them to a functioning computer."

"Maybe. Have you ever had corrupted files before?"

"No, this is the first time."

"Talk to Jon tomorrow. Maybe he can scrape up the funds for a new computer."

She stuffs the cube back into her front pocket, where the corners dig her thigh again. She wonders if her leg has begun to form a permanent divot for the gadget to rest from the many times it has hibernated in her pocket.

"Well, I'm done doing what I meant to do," Abby says, "so I'm going to take off. Are you done here, or are you staying?"

Byron puts down his little hammer. He was flattening one of the red panels the whole time she was talking. Unlike the little blue panel, the red one makes no sound.

"The trick is in the metal," he states, ignoring her question. He raises the panel to eye level, peering at it with one eye squeezed shut.

"The what now?"

"The trick is in the metal you choose and how you form it. The kits are secondary."

"O-kay, so where do the panels come from?"

"Not here," Byron says, examining an untouched panel.

"All right, well, do you know what they are made of?" she says, irritated.

"Nope. No one does."

"Don't we have ways of testing that? I mean, I'm putting trust in what people ship to my lab."

"We should, but we don't. Usual methods are...inconclusive. We, as inventors, are here to put these panels to use to see what they can become. Who knows? They could be little ticking time bombs."

"Um, what?" She glares at him, her voice flat.

"Well, kid, what did you think your job was?"

Abby throws her hands up in the air. "After hearing this *grand* revelation, I guess I really don't know!"

Abby stays with Byron until he decides he's ready to leave, which isn't much longer. They make their way out of B6, back toward daylight.

Abby checks her watch. "It's only three p.m. Do you think I should try to find Tyler and see if I can reverse his sickness?"

"Do you know where he lives?" Byron raises an eyebrow.

"Yes, he wrote his address down for me when I dropped him off the other day. I think it's on a napkin in my glove bo—"

A crash rings through the atrium. Abby shields her head with her forearm underneath Byron's wide arm, which has also shot out to cover her head. A naked Tyler bursts through the front door, spraying several shards of black glass, and he rolls with a wet thump in front of them. Soto's alarm squeals through the air as he rises high on two tentacles and turns his human head to face the duo. His eyes lock on Abby. Several pallid tentacles thrash behind him, cracking the floor tiles and swiping everything off the abandoned front desk. Abby takes a staccato step back, her limbs frozen and mouth open. She grips Byron's wrist tightly, and he flexes under her fingers.

"T-tyler?" Abby's voice cracks.

The sound of her voice sends him into a primal lust, and his gaze focuses intently on her. Abby begins to hum, her fingers scrabbling at her tight front pocket, which is stuffed with the cube.

Tyler is too fast for her. He rushes her with inhuman speed, wrapping one free tentacle around her neck and choking out her song. A second fat tentacle grabs her around the waist. Her pocket hand lifts and tenses, knocking her badge to the floor, where it clatters, echoing in the atrium. Tyler lifts her and turns back toward the hole he created in the side of the building.

"Hey!" Byron runs toward him, but he's thrown aside by a third appendage, sending him soaring through the atrium to land hard against a wall. Byron slumps over, closing his eyes. Slime coats his face and beard and oozes from the tip of his nose.

Chapter 10

Hunter

In a daze, Byron shakes his head after being hurled against the wall between the two bathrooms. He gets up fast, feeling the fog of faint the blow knocked into his head. He stumbles and rubs the back of his head to feel a lump already swollen into an egg. Looking at his palm, he sees no blood and sighs in relief.

He shakes his head again, hoping it will bring the world back into focus. Nausea bubbles in his stomach, and he stumbles to take a deep breath, clutching his abdomen. The reality of a severe concussion begins to sink in. Looking back up, he sees specks of dust and oddly ethereal glimmers of microscopic glass particles swirling in the new beam of sunlight now radiating into the building. Other shards of glass lay scattered across the floor, reflecting beautiful patterns inside the once cold and sterile atrium. He wills away the nausea and closes his eyes for a moment to steady his throbbing skull.

The darkness swirls behind his eyelids. He wants to fall over.

"Snap out of it, By," he says, returning his thick hand to the lump. He opens his eyes again, the glass and dust motes swirling into focus. He trots toward the squid-shaped opening to the outside, hoping his stomach will remain settled.

Byron's heart pounds hard but steadily in his chest. He examines the land before him, looking for signs of the monster. The air is quiet save for the sighing trees in the distance. He limps to Abby's small car, taking note of the twinge in his knee. He looks around, careful not to rock his brain, and stops when he spots a palm-size chunk of pavement that has worked its way loose from the parking lot. He fists the chunk and chucks it at Abby's car window. The force sends another wave of nausea through his gut.

Her window shatters into little shards that tinkle down the side of her passenger door. Reaching inside, he lifts the handle, and the door swings open. Scanning the seats, floor, and console, he comes up empty. Popping open the glove box, a beige napkin flutters out of the compartment, covered in wrinkled, wet stains. There's the address. He grabs the napkin and looks at Tyler's scrawling: *78 Circle Point off Ashcroft.*

He folds the napkin and tucks it into his back pocket. A glint from the compartment catches his eye. He peers back into the glovebox to see a slick black 0.45 caliber pistol.

"Good girl," Byron smirks. He swipes the gun and checks the clip. Six rounds, empty chamber. He flips the safety on and tucks the gun into his waistband, telling himself not to shoot his balls off.

As he limps away from her car, the bright light burns his fragile vision, and he struggles to focus, putting his hand up in salute to block out the sun. He fumbles around in his pocket for the keys to his pickup truck. His thumb jams down on the arming button, and his truck beeps in response. Byron labors toward the sound of the beeps as he repeatedly presses the alarm button. His eyes continue to adjust to the bright light while scanning the area around him for signs of the menace.

The beeping finally leads him to the truck. Byron can see that the peeling light-blue bed has a deep dent across the width and a shattered back windshield. He curses under his breath, figuring Tyler used the bed as leverage with one of his twisted tentacles to propel himself faster down the lot.

Byron sees that everything else seems to be in order with his truck, including fully functional tires that aren't flat. He jumps into the driver's side. The smell of vintage fabric mingled with fresh air flowing in from the broken back window fills his nose and his will with renewed vigor. The truck growls to life at the turn of his key, with no unusual lights on the dash to indicate mechanical damage. He sighs heavily with great relief and surveys the lot for any sign of Tyler's trail.

Tyler's side-winding tentacle trail and Abby's dragging feet lead into the forest by the utility road. Bare footprints press into the dirt in the middle of the smooth grooves left by the tentacles. Byron is already way behind in the chase—no trace of Tyler, only the prints left behind. He revs the engine and spins out in the direction of the trail. The carved ground weaves up and around as he drives through the utility road.

In a slick motion, he slides out his phone and calls Ben, who doesn't answer. He's not sure why, but he calls Jon next.

"Byron, what do you need?" Jon's voice comes through, sounding tired.

"We have a situation."

There's a silent pause. "What do you mean?"

"Tough to explain. I need you to meet me at the north utility road."

Byron's tires protest against the grass and mud, spraying thick water against the bramble.

"What do you need?"

"I'm not sure yet."

"Be there in a few minutes." Jon hangs up.

Ben calls back as Byron is about to put down his phone. "Hey, Byron, Sorry I missed you. What's up?"

"Abby is in trouble," Byron spits.

"What do you mean?"

"I mean, that good ol' boy accountant friend of hers is a mutated creep, and he just burst into Soto an' stole her."

Silence.

"Ben?" Byron finally asks.

"I'm sorry... What?"

"Start makin' your way to Soto Labs—you don't live far, right? Make your way, and I'll meet you on the north utility road. Be quick—leave now!" Byron hangs up.

He continues winding through the dense forest cluster, bouncing hard on the mud and rock of the utility road. Wet earth splatters high around the truck from the velocity, but his eyes remain focused on the smooth, wet tentacle tracks carved in front of him. After several minutes, the break in the trees starts to grow as the utility road meets the main road. Byron screeches to a halt, spraying more mud before throwing the truck into park to wait for Ben. The engine *putt-putts* puffs of vapor as it idles.

Byron taps his fingers on the steering wheel, whipping his head around for any sign of another vehicle. Rather than the modest blue sedan that Ben drives, a small silver sports car quickly approaches up the hill to Byron's left. Its tires squeal to a stop next to the utility road as the driver notices Byron's truck. A tinted window slides down to reveal Tony's smug face in the passenger seat. Behind the wheel is Jon, bending over to get a look at Byron.

"He insisted on coming," Jon shouts out the window.

Byron glares at Tony.

"We were having a private meeting down the road." Jon shrugs. "So, what do you need?"

Byron nods and points a thick, calloused finger at a swollen slime trail on the pavement, punched down in spots from other vehicles that had driven over it. The path veers sharply back into the forest on the other side of the road.

Jon follows Byron's finger to rest his eyes on the markings. After a few seconds, his face scrunches, and his neck recoils.

"What the hell am I looking at?" He squints and blinks in an attempt to believe what he's seeing. Tony tilts his head toward the trail, gaze unfaltering and blank.

Jon gets out of the car and jogs over to the trail, looking left and right for any sudden traffic. He stares at it momentarily before slowly crouching to dip a finger in the ooze. Byron gets out of his truck to join Jon, but Tony stays planted in Jon's luxury interior, his arms crossed.

Jon plays with the slime between thumb and forefinger when Byron approaches, assessing its foul viscosity. .

"That's probably not the best idea," Byron suggests as Jon brings the covered finger to his nose for a smell.

"Byron, what is this? Why is there so much of it, and to whom—or what—does it belong?"

Byron sighs at the barrage of questions and tells him about Tyler. While explaining Metaxysm, he hears tires crunching over the gravel on the shoulder behind his car.

The vehicle stops, and Ben gets out of his blue sedan. He approaches the pair. They have moved to the shoulder once again, and Jon is scrubbing a finger through a handkerchief. Ben looks over as he passes Jon's car to see Tony in the passenger seat, sitting still with his arms crossed and wearing a bored expression.

"What's going on?" Ben peels his gaze from Tony back to Byron and Jon.

"Abby's in trouble," Byron says.

"What did you mean when you said Tyler 'stole' her? And what about all this mutated creep talk?"

Byron tells Ben about Abby's invention but is interrupted by a buzz coming from Ben's pocket. He whips out his phone and sees a glowing text from Abby.

Abby P. 3:55 p.m.: Cvirclke Poiuntr

"What does that mean?" Ben asks the group.

Byron pulls the napkin from his pocket and unfolds it for Ben. He taps the address.

"Circle Point! She said Tyler wrote down his address for her, and this is it. This is where he took her."

"Should we call the cops?" asks Ben.

"No, no cops," Jon steps forward, waving his hands low.

"Why not?"

"If this is what you say it is, this is a Soto matter."

"A Soto matter? You think Soto is above the law or something?" Ben cocks an eyebrow.

"No, but there are certain... 'rules' in place," he says. Ben knows Jon isn't telling the truth. There's more to this than just rules.

"The longer we wait, the more trouble Abby is in," Byron says, handing the napkin to Jon.

"Well, we'd better hurry then." Jon takes the napkin and jogs back to his car. "We have no idea what that thing might do to her."

Chapter 11

DISTURBED

TYLER MOVES WITH INCREDIBLE speed. Abby claws at the tentacle squeezing her neck—her fingers continually slip and scrabble for purchase on the slick surface of the soft flesh. Her legs dangle, occasionally striking the forest floor and threatening to break her ankles. She wriggles her torso from inside the grip of the other appendage to try to hold her legs up, but Tyler's erratic moves continue to thrash her bones.

Her eyes dart around her surroundings, the light fading in and out of her view. Off in the distance, she spots a weathered tent with two men lying in the grass. Abby tries again to make space between her throat and the undulating alien flesh to scream out for help, but all she can muster is a hoarse hissing sound.

As the two weave through the forest, small branches and bits of bramble strike her face and legs. The heat from the lashings makes her cheeks throb. Feeling the blood pulsing behind her eyes, she closes them.

This is the day I die. And I deserve it.

Her mind reels at what she did. Her failed invention, infused with her own blood, mingling with Tyler's alcohol, and merging with the contents of his gut from lunch, must have been the source of this transformation. She's sure of it. Blindly, she reaches into her front pocket, where the new gadget rests innocently, waiting for another activation. All she feels is cold, wet rubber.

Would it even work on him? Why couldn't I just carry a purse?

More brambles slash her ankles.

My phone... she remembers.

Opening her eyes once more to see if Tyler notices her, she only sees his gaze pressing forward. She reaches behind her to feel for an opening. There it is- a space between the tentacle and her back has exposed her back pocket and the phone tucked neatly inside it. She grazes the fabric with a light touch and then stops.

Wait for the right moment, she tells herself, as any bump would knock the thing out of her grasp and most certainly spell her doom. She closes her eyes and prays for the right moment.

Tyler halts at the edge of the forest. The extra tentacles undulate behind him as if caught in a light breeze while he once again stands on two human feet. His eyes zero in on the cluster of buildings in front of him: Circle Point Apartments.

Abby uses this moment to reach into her back pocket. She swipes without abandon, finding Ben at the top of her contacts. She begins to punch out the words, but Tyler goes on the move again, slower this time, but not without turbulence. She fat-fingers an attempt to type out the name of the complex.

Tyler stares down at her and sees the phone in her hand. The cube's effects have taken a toll on his appearance. The once-crystalline color of his eyes, which she found oddly pleasant, has turned dark, with bloodied whites sunk deep into purple sockets. She taps the "send" button while glaring back at him.

The guttural, inhuman growl that bubbles from his throat sends chills down Abby's spine. He flicks the phone from her hand, and it soars through the air, landing with a crunch in the parking lot in front of them. Abby could only hope the message was sent before the phone cracked on the pavement.

The naked man moves once again, scanning for neighbors. A door opens on the bottom floor, causing Tyler to race to his own unit. The octopus body squirms and rolls to the building. Abby sees the stooped woman shuffle out of her door from the downstairs apartment. Once again, she attempts to pry her neck free from the tentacle in a desperate cry for help, but her fingers slip and fail with no time to spare as Tyler dodges the old woman's glance up the stairs and around the corner.

***

Ben's sedan and Byron's truck screech to a halt next to each other in the parking lot of Circle Point Apartments, building seven. Jon rolls up next to them.

"Why would he come to his own apartment? Isn't this a little... obvious?" Ben asks, slamming his door.

"You didn't see the guy," Byron says. "He didn't look like he was the thinking type if you know what I mean. Do you have a weapon?"

Byron pats the front of his pants, where the gun bulges.

"Ah, I think so!" Ben jogs to his passenger side and pulls out a four-inch blade hidden in a red sheath.

"No, I don't carry *weapons*," Tony remarks with disdain, pushing Jon's door closed with a foot.

"Sorry. I don't have one either," Jon says.

"Then we need to make sure to use these wisely," Byron says, "and I have a feeling this won't be easy."

"If Tyler has become what you said he is, who's to say Abby's still alive?" Tony picks at his fingers and then spits on the ground.

Ben and Byron glare at Tony while Jon stares at the apartment building.

"Hey, I think I see where the trail continues," Jon says, shielding his eyes and pointing toward the building.

Their eyes follow his hand to see the slime tracks winding through the grass up to building seven.

Ben pauses for a moment, remembering the other thing he had stashed in a rage in one of his crusted cup holders. "Hold on. Wait for me," he says.

He returns to his sedan and pops open the passenger door. Leaning to the center console, he sees the glint of red shimmering there, the top of a bald dome peeking over the side of a well. He wraps his fingers around it, feeling its cold surface in his palm. He stuffs it into his front pocket.

***

Tyler carries Abby to the end of the hall. He flicks the door, and it splits at the jamb, popping open and bouncing off the wall. The door stopper twangs violently, the noise echoing through the room.

The tentacles slither over the floor and furniture, which are already coated with explosions of hazy secretions. He carries Abby toward the bedroom at the back of the apartment. He helps himself through the door with fat tentacles, leaving more drippings over the trim. Peering into the bathroom, Abby glances at the black carnage within. Splatters of vomit and excrement cover the walls and floor. A pile of clothes lies crumpled and crusted amid the mess—they're the clothes Tyler wore to work on Friday. Abby remembered the pale lavender button-up and khaki pants, now soiled beyond repair.

Tyler's mangled features search the area. Not finding what he's looking for, he slides to the other room across the hall. There, in the closet, she sees it. An undulating mass of black bubbles. Her presence in the room causes the mass to chitter and gnash.

Tenderly, he sets her on the floor, then unwraps her neck and slides a moist tip over her cheek.

"Chhilldrennnnn," Tyler gurgles from deep within his throat. His tongue forks outward toward Abby between small teeth. "Mothher rrr..."

She opens her mouth to speak when Tyler thrusts a tentacle against her face, filling her mouth with a thick, slippery ooze. Her head smacks against the wall, and she rolls her eyes back, heaving slime from her throat. The flavor of metal and rotting flesh coats her taste buds——a cheesy concoction from hell that she tries to expel with a wriggling tongue.

A jelly blob slides to the back of her throat. She feels the bile rise in her gut, threatening to spew forth with nowhere to go other than back down her throat. As tears trickle from her eyes, she lets out a pleading groan. The blob slides down the back of her tongue; she feels it plunk into her stomach, the cold trail haunting her esophagus. The feeling makes her gag and gurgle.

The writhing mass begins to break apart, revealing small black beasts the size of basketballs. Their tentacles slap and crawl toward Abby.

She clutches Tyler's tentacle, attempting to pry it from her mouth so she can vomit, but the suckers squeeze against her lips, refusing to give. A few of the beasts make their way to her, crawling into her lap and running their dark legs over her face. One of them slithers into the crook of her arm as if waiting for her to feed it. It makes little sucking noises at her, sharp rows of teeth clicking. Others crawl all over her, leaving their own slime trails and feeling her face and bare arms.

Abby's body shakes. The sucking noises from the beast in her arms ignite a fury within her. *If I can get up fast enough to pry Metaxysm from my pocket before Tyler knocks me down again...*

She calculates her move as black arms plant over her eyes and nose. The soft, squishy feel of their legs discovering all the crevices on her face makes her want to gag all over again. More beasts crawl on her. *Suck, suck, suck.*

I'll distract him, she thinks.

Tyler looks at her with a gaping red grin. She wraps both hands around the sucking creature and squeezes them together. With the rage of ten men, she chucks the beast across the room. Tyler watches his child soar through the air before hitting the wall and bursting like a water balloon, spraying the wall with black blood. He removes the tentacle from her mouth to slither over to his broken child.

Abby jumps up, knocking the rest of the beasts from her body. She jams a fist into her pocket, wrapping her fingers around the sharp object. She opens her mouth to sing, but her body heaves, and she vomits a stream of secretions. The splatter grabs the attention of Tyler, who turns back to Abby. She spits the rest of the slime from her mouth and looks up to see Tyler slithering back to her.

She wails just before he pins her against the wall by the neck. Then he jabs a tentacle back over her mouth and wraps her in a twisted cocoon to lift her up. His sunken black eyes get close to hers, and she sees a glimmer of the crystalline color they once were, buried deep underneath liquid onyx. He stays there, glaring at her, the onyx orbs moving up and down across her face.

***

Ben, Byron, Jon, and Tony follow the slime trail. An older, stooped woman sprays the walkway, washing away the ooze, which forms jellyfish globs that swim down the stream into the sewer. She smiles under a hairy lip and gives them a feeble wave. Ben responds with a millisecond nod before turning back on the path, not wanting to initiate small talk.

"I didn't know this young dude lived in an old folks' retirement center," Byron says.

"It's not an old folks' home. It's more of a high-class apartment complex," Ben responds.

"It certainly is quiet around here," Jon admits just before the sound of a wail and a crash come from a few floors above.

The men stop and stare upward. Ben jolts up the stairs, with Byron close behind, followed by Jon and Tony. More slime clings to the guardrail until the fourth floor, where it stops. Ben creeps through the hallway, his ears pricked for any hint of sound. Byron is hunched, looking around and guarding Ben's back. Jon marches to meet up with Ben. Clattering sounds come from near the end of the hall.

"Look, here..." Jon points at the second-to-last door. It's cracked open about an inch, with wood splinters splayed around the jamb.

"Apartment seventy-eight," Byron says. "This has to be it."

The hinges creak as Ben pushes the door open.

"Disgusting," Tony says, looking around at the slime coating the room.

"Ugh, the smell." Ben scrunches his nose.

A clattering noise comes from the back of the apartment. They see a large shadow dart across the hall.

Byron turns to Ben. "Are you a good shot?"

"I'm okay. Why?"

"I'm *not* a good shot. Trade me weapons. There are six bullets in the clip."

"Damn it, Byron." Ben pulls out the knife and hands it handle first to Byron.

Ben checks the safety and tucks the pistol into his waistband. He gives Byron a look and starts to tiptoe through the front room with Byron right behind him, then Jon and Tony. Their feet slip over the floor, making Tony twist an ankle and curse under his breath.

Shadows play on the wall at the end of the hall. Long strips of undulating shadow puppets beckon them. The men approach, their footfalls making eerie squelching sounds over the messy carpet. The first doorway leads to a bright guest bath with clean whites and ivories decorating the interior. *Squish, squish, squish.* A faint rattling noise comes from the room at the end of the hall.

The hairs on Ben's neck prickle, and he backs into the wall, sliding across the drywall, the other men following his lead. They pass the second open doorway. It appears to be a guest area, but it's empty, save for a squirming pile of individual black balls that rise up and down in unison in the center of the room like a boiling cauldron. Ben freezes in place, motioning for the others to stop. He puts a finger to his lips to signal for quiet.

The balls also freeze in place with the group, sensing their heat. Their tiny faces turn toward the men, little black eyes bulging and staring. The beast on top slingshots itself at Ben.

He puts his hands up fast, blocking the creature from sinking its razor-sharp teeth into his neck. Instead, the thing gets his hand, blood spraying from the wound and making Ben grunt low in silent pain. Byron tries to grab the creature, his hands sliding over its slick hide. Their shoes squeal in the slime as they wrestle the slippery creature. Jon spreads his arms behind him to guard Tony. Rather than stand still, Tony ducks under Jon's arms and squelches over to the pair. He digs his fingertips into its sides for greater purchase and squeezes. The creature lets out a high-pitched squeal, releasing Ben's hand. Tony sends the thing flying back into the empty guest room, where it lands perfectly on the pile, scattering the rest of the creatures like marbles. Byron pushes Tony out of the way and grabs the door handle, pulling it shut as several beasts slam their bodies against it.

Their attack sounds like little tennis balls hitting the wood. After thirty seconds, the noises die down. A pool of blackness creeps from the crack under the door, snaking around the soles of Tony's white sneakers. He wrinkles his nose and lifts his feet one at a time, inching back to the opposite wall, where Ben is pressed and holding his hand.

Jon looks at the door and the puddle of oil sliding from beneath it. Eyes closed, Tony presses against the wall, his sweaty palms gripping the drywall.

Ben looks at the punctures in his hand. The holes well up and drip dark venous blood. His fingers begin to contort and crack, balling into a fist he struggles to pry open. *Is it poison?* he frantically wonders.

His arm goes limp, turning to stone as the muscles twitch and freeze. He quickly jams the unbitten hand into his pocket, feeling the small red orb. Activating the button causes it to warm up and pulse healing energy through his veins. Ben eyeballs Tony to ensure his eyes remain closed while he heals himself. Byron stares at him from underneath bushy eyebrows, a knowing look in his rheumy eyes.

Ben's chest heaves while the puncture wounds close. He rips the sleeve of his dead arm to create a makeshift bandage and hides the fresh skin from Tony and Jon. His long scar wrinkles and glistens with his movements. The arm remains limp and frozen, but at least it's no longer pumping creeping poison into his blood. He releases a heavy sigh, rolling his head over to look at Tony. Tony looks back at him; a sweat slick has broken over his brow, matting the wispy hairs he has left over his temples. He gives a slight nod to Ben, who nods back and swallows.

After a short pause, Ben points a thumb to the door behind him, motioning for the rest to follow him inside. The three of them nod, acknowledging the gesture, and wait for his move.

Ben rolls to the side, attempting to peek into the bedroom. Shadows continue to be cast against the far wall of the hallway, occasionally playing over Byron's arm as he remains planted against the guest room door. Ben can't see much. He slides the pistol from his waistband, the steel pulling against bare flesh, which is warm and sticky from the rush of blood beneath his skin. He points it upward at his side, leaving the safety on just in case.

Seeing this, Byron grips the knife, still sheathed in its red casing, and points it downward. Ben's other arm remains limp at his side. Knowing he can only rely on the good arm, he swallows and closes his eyes for a heartbeat before stepping inside the bedroom; gun pointed forward.

A large undulating idol stands before him— the black silhouette against an orange sun setting from behind.

"I ha-ave bee-een waiiittinnng," Tyler growls at the men. Hardened scales quiver over his neck, making the soft rattle they heard earlier.

He stands with his back to the window. Light pours in from the window panels, passing through Tyler's translucent yellow skin with swirling pus under the surface. Red-black veins grip various body parts as if holding them together while a dark cluster of organs pump wildly under the surface. Boils coat the surface of his face, rising and falling like heavy breaths.

Abby stands petrified at his side, tears in her eyes and a tentacle pulsing around her neck and mouth. Her hands flex open and shake.

The bedroom is big for an apartment. The bed has been thrown against the wall, the crooked mattress pressing against the surface and close to tipping back over. Dust and shards of wood and glass litter the floor. Byron's boots crunch over the debris, followed by Tony and Jon.

"Hey, Tyler," Ben says, not knowing why.

Tyler bends his neck to see around Ben. His animalistic movements remind Ben of a cat.

"Youuuu," Tyler hisses.

The four men exchange glances, unsure of who the monster refers to. Byron grips the knife tighter.

Tony steps out from behind Ben, arms up in a field goal position.

"Tony, get back," Jon whispers, reaching for the back of Tony's shirt.

"Are you talking to me?" Tony asks hands still in the air.

Tyler's bloodied eyes follow Tony as he sidesteps Ben and rounds closer.

"Look, I can fix you, buddy. Don't worry." Tony's voice warbles; Ben isn't sure whether he's unafraid or terrified.

"Yyouuu are the Tooe-neeee." Tyler's tongue flicks out from beneath yellowed teeth, blood sliding over their surfaces.

"Yes, I am Tony," he says, looking at Abby. She stares at him with tears in her eyes. She tries to shake her head to get him to back off, but he looks back at Tyler.

"If you just come back to the lab, I can heal whatever this is."

Tony arcs his hands in front of him like a rainbow as if trying to magic away Tyler's affliction. He planks a hand out to Tyler as a truce gesture.

Tyler's eyes glide over the group of men in front of him, searching. His gaze pauses on Byron, knife in hand.

A tentacle pulses forward, grabbing Byron's arm before he can react. The flesh slides, coiling down his arm in a microsecond, lifting the knife from his grip and squeezing around the handle. Byron attempts to reach out and steal the blade back but merely grabs the red holster and falls backward with the empty scabbard in his palm.

The serrated blade flashes across Ben's vision, whipping to his right and finding a home in Tony's jugular. Tony gurgles and sprays blood from his lips. His eyes bulge while helpless hands reach up to his neck, finding the slick flesh still gripping the handle, and the hard blade sunk deep into his own. He tries to say something, but more blood pulses from his mouth. The gash drips thick blood down his shirt.

Tyler rips the blade to the side, slicing through half the neck. Tony's eyes glaze over, and his arms fall to his sides. His knees buckle, and he crumples to the floor. Abby lets out a muffled squeal. She looks down at Tony's balding pate, now slathered in red, his head glued to the rest of his body only by the remaining chunk of his neck.

Shredded red meat pumps more blood onto the floor, slowing and pooling around his lifeless body.

Jon rushes to Tony. Tyler picks him up by the waist with another tentacle, squeezing hard. Jon coughs and vomits as Tyler flings him toward the window. His back hits the glass, and it shatters, allowing a hot breeze to fill the room. A soft thump can be heard as Jon's body breaks into jelly on the pavement outside.

Ben can't move. His eyes lock on Tony's face—eyes rolled back, and mouth parted in a soundless scream. *Just like Holly.*

Rage bubbles inside him. His arm, limp from the poison and scarred from his youth, hangs by his side as the tentacles sway in front of him. Tyler's human hand is now gripping the blade, claiming it for his own as he grins at the remaining pair with cracked lips.

Byron crouches low, armed only with an empty scabbard and clammy hands. His eyes dart from Abby to Ben and Tyler. The tentacle squeezes Abby's face tighter, and she tries to gag.

Ben fixes the gun back on Tyler; his hand shakes, and sweat drips from his brow. "Tyler," he says through gritted teeth.

From deep within his throat, Tyler bellows an otherworldly screech. The hardened flaps sculpted on his neck shudder and quake, filling the room with an alien cacophony. Abby lets out a small "urk" as the tentacle continues to squeeze her neck.

Tyler moves his face to Abby's and takes a deep breath of her scent. She jams her eyes shut, a single tear squeezing out as she shakes. He presses his mouth to her cheek, the forked tongue flicking over her skin. His hot breath, stinking of bile and rot, fills her nose, worse than the memory of his sickness in her car Friday night. The throat clacks, and the neck scales shudder again.

For Ben, time could be moving backward or forward at light speed. Everything is spinning around him, and his brain screams at the carnage. He scans the room and notices something about Abby. Her fist is jammed in her pocket. She fidgets her knuckles around under the fabric. As Tyler whips his tentacles through the room in a tantrum, she draws her hand out, clutching something between locked fingers. She turns her hand, opening her palm to reveal a sliver of the delicate cube in her grip. Red lines have dug into her palm, leaking a small amount of her blood, which sucks into the gadget. Her eyes roll over to Byron.

The cube hums in her hand, an eerie mechanical sound from another world. Ben looks at Byron, who's still crouched in the corner, holding the side of his head and locking eyes with Abby.

The gun remains poised in his hand. *There's no round in the chamber.* His thumb shakes as he clicks the safety off. He then looks back at Abby's watery eyes, Metaxysm dancing in her shaking palm. Ben knows he must make a choice.

Ben attempts to shoot Tyler:
Turn to Chapter "Investigator." (Page 147)

Ben tries to use Metaxysm:
Turn to Chapter "Paralysis." (Page 163)

Ben rushes Tyler with brute force:
Turn to Chapter "Creeps." (Page 177)

investigator

Ben has chosen to shoot Tyler

USING HIS LIMP HAND as leverage, Ben wriggles the slide under his fingers and tries to chamber the round. Although the slide is stiff, he's able to cock it back.

He points the barrel at Tyler's yellow, pus-filled torso and squeezes the trigger. *Click. Click.*

Tyler is distracted by Abby. His scaly neck buzzes like a snake as his black eyes pore over every inch of her. He unhinges his jaw, emitting another primal scream. *Click, click.*

Ben curses under his breath and smacks the gun against his leg. Ben thinks he can hear Byron's deep voice but can't tell what he's saying—adrenaline pounds at his eardrums.

The smacking sounds grab Tyler's attention this time. He growls deep from his belly and hurls Abby across the room, where she hits the wall hard. The drywall bursts open, spraying a dust cloud around her. Tyler slithers at Ben as he pounds the barrel's side against his thigh.

Byron leaps forward in front of Ben, knocking him over and landing on top of him while Tyler's tentacles slap and pound the floor and walls. Byron grunts and coughs hard, spraying blood from his mouth. Ben feels Byron's warmth soaking into his jeans as he remains pinned underneath the large square of a man. He feels the steel of the gun still loosely held in his grip as his knuckles press against the hardwood floor. Tyler's black eyes bore into Ben's, daring him to move as the human hand slowly withdraws, revealing the serrated edge ripping its way back out of Byron's belly. Byron groans as the blade cuts its way back out of his flesh.

Ben feels lost. He's trapped underneath nearly 250 pounds of his dying colleague, with who knows how much weight of another. The pressure pushes down on his midsection, causing his eyes to bulge and heat to fill his face. His eyes bounce from friend to friend and living enemy to fallen enemy. Byron's heartbeat pounds hard and slows as he lies face-up, gurgling. Tony's corpse lies crumpled in a corner, no longer plagued by competition. The hole in the shattered window, letting in the warm breeze, holds the impetus of Jon's demise and broken body lying on the red sidewalk below. Abby sits against the wall, hunched over and semi-unconscious. Deep red bruises encircle her small neck. Her body heaves with silent coughs when she finally looks up, terrified veined eyes locking with Ben's.

You have to learn how to take risks! Abby's voice echoes in his skull.

A large, languid palm reaches down to feel for the slide of the gun. In a dying effort to help, Byron's weakened meaty fingers wrap around the slide. Using a combination of Byron's remaining strength and Ben's pinned-down hand, he cocks the chamber, releasing a cluster of dead rounds.

Ben looks back up at Tyler, a monstrosity mixed of man and animal. Tiny human hands dwarfed by the size of alien tentacles clutch the knife coated in Byron's blood. He raises the sullied blade above Ben's head in line to plunge it directly into the prime meridian of his skull. Tyler's eyes are crazed, but his motions are jittery; Ben could swear the creature is fighting with himself. He points the barrel of the .45 caliber straight at Tyler's forehead and closes his eyes.

God help me...

Click. Bang!

The alien face explodes into a mess of teeth and hair. The shot rings in Ben's ears in a high-pitched wail as a yellow shower of pus mixed with blackened blood rains over Ben and Byron. Tyler's hands go slack, dropping to his side. The blade clacks to the floor, barely missing Ben's leg. The room is deafeningly quiet until Tyler's body slides sideways and thumps to the floor.

Abby rocks her head to blink at the pair. She rises on shaking legs to dust herself off, then limps toward the men, holding her arm. She looks at the pile of bodies in the room: one alive, one barely alive, and two clearly dead.

"Guys..." Byron coughs out, spitting out another mouthful of blood. "Are you okay?" His voice is weak and far away.

Abby hurries over to him and kneels on the floor beside him. "Yes, Byron, we're okay. Save your strength. We'll get you help, don't worry." Her bloodshot eyes struggle for moisture as she tends to him, frantically placing her hands on his stomach in an attempt to squish his intestines back into his body. Ben pats Byron from underneath.

"The cops will be here soon for sure," Abby croaks, "Someone will find Jon out there any minute now."

"You saved my life," Ben tells Byron.

Byron grins wide and red, lifting his head to look at the wound. His weakened muscles fight for a drop of strength. He grunts and drops his head back to the floor.

Abby's lip trembles as she looks at her dying friend. Sadness flips to rage when she looks at Tyler's body, still warm and half-draped over Byron. She grunts and kicks Tyler hard enough that he rolls over and thuds to the floor. His face is unrecognizable. The handsome, dusty-blond-haired man who began to scratch her itch for companionship has transformed into a nightmare. The once-chiseled jaw has become mush, with black blood oozing from torn yellow flesh, his crooked nose peeking out from a row of mangled top teeth. Tentacles are spread throughout the room, lying still and coiled around various objects. She averts her eyes to avoid Tyler's nakedness.

"If only we had Tony's stupid gadget..." She kicks a piece of drywall, putting a hand to her head in pain.

Ben jerks his head up and pats his pocket. "Abby, help me up!"

Abby crouches, grabbing Byron's wrists and tugging him forward. Byron groans again. Ben slips out from underneath him and helps his head back down to the floor.

"I brought Knitting Sphere!" Ben says, jamming his hand into his pocket and pulling out the unremarkable small red orb.

Abby swipes the sphere, smashes the little button, and crams it into Byron's palm, folding his fingers over it and holding it in place with her own hands.

You shouldn't bring a prototype outside the lab, Ben's chastisement echoes in her mind. She's grateful he didn't take his own advice.

"Please work, please work," she chants.

His intestines are hanging outside his body.

Abby places her forehead on Byron's beefy fist. While she weeps and repeats her mantra, the familiar warmth spreads over her brow from Byron's fingers. She rears back to see the same biological glow, showcasing red vessels and bones. The effects travel up through Byron's arm, waking him from his pain. The trio watches as the light travels through his body until it settles around the wet opening that splits his belly button in two. The brightness intensifies, illuminating the edges of torn flesh and sending pinholes of light from capillaries.

Byron lets out an animalistic howl. Ben and Abby watch in awe as the blood that sprayed from the wound creates a reverse fountain of red back into his body. A small portion of his small intestine that was poking out of the wound jolts to life, then slithers back inside the gash, causing the big man to emit another low groan.

"What are you doing to me?" he screams at the pair, who have been watching the gruesome reversal in a morbid trance. They say nothing to him.

Byron wails again when the flesh around the wound moves on its own accord as if a thousand maggots are squirming under the surface. It then begins to glue itself back together.

The sphere completes its job, finalizing the reversal as the glow dims. The wound closes up entirely, as if it had never existed, only evidenced by the hole that remains in Byron's shirt.

He jolts upright, looking at the hole. After handing the sphere back to Ben, he fumbles around with the fabric, feeling around at the skin underneath in shock. "Was that *your* gadget?" he asks Ben.

"Yeah, an idea Tony stole." Ben looks back at Tony's lifeless form. *He's clearly dead. There's no way to save him with this.*

"Well, I'll be damned. That was just as painful as getting stabbed." Byron laughs.

Abby can't peel her eyes off Tony. She suddenly feels sad for him despite how awful he was in life. Ben sits on the floor next to Byron, looking at Tyler's naked body and mangled face.

"Do you think it's over?"

Abby studies Ben, her sad expression morphing into one of fear. A cold sweat burns her forehead as the pit in her stomach grows. "What do you mean?"

"What about those creatures in the guest bedroom?"

Abby's eyes go wide, and she sucks in a sharp breath.

Byron grunts as he rolls to this side to get up. He limps over debris and a wad of tentacles to look out the window. Jon's body lies on the pavement, sides split in two. An older woman in slippers and night attire walks her little terrier with a pink leash and bells on the collar. She shuffles curiously toward Jon's body and lets out a bloodcurdling wail.

"Cops will definitely be here soon now," he says.

Ben looks down and gives one of the tentacles a good kick; it flops over, revealing rows of tiny black buds. He bends down to get a better look at the strange growths coming from the appendage. They look like little marbles, still deep but emerging, ready to pop out if given a good squeeze. Looking around, he picks up the knife that was about to split his brain in half and uses the point to poke at a bud. It gives easily under the pressure of the knife's tip. More dark blood drips from the spot, trickling down the blade to mingle with Byron's fluid. The little poke sends a trigger to the rest of the row, and they all begin to drop like ripe fruit and plunk to the floor. One of the buds unravels, revealing itself to the room. Minuscule tentacles unfurl from the marble, showing off a tiny face and shiny black eyes. The little thing splits open, showing rows of small, pointed black teeth.

Ben jumps back, gripping his limp arm. "Don't touch those!" he shouts. More buds drop from Tyler's tentacles, hitting the floor in a cacophony of soft thuds. They all unravel to reveal an audience of swaying tentacles and black eyes.

Abby walks toward him when she sees all the little fruits lying on the floor. She lets out a gasp and leaps back.

"So that's where they came from..." Her voice trails off.

Ben pokes at another one with the dagger. It doesn't respond, letting the point sink into it with ease. "This one just let me stab it." He stands back up.

"The blast to Tyler's face must have severed the life source for these little dudes, making them die," Byron says.

Abby stares at the little creatures lying there, several faces staring back up at her with those familiar black eyes and teeth. *Suck, suck, suck.* She shudders.

"Rebirth..." Abby whispers. Byron looks up at her.

"What does that mean?" Ben asks.

"Remember? There was Excitement, then Passion...which we don't need to discuss. Transmogrification was next, which is obvious here. Then *Rebirth*.

"This morning, I made a new Metaxysm to correct the one Tyler dropped into his drink. It was complete with the last two attributes—Melody and Rectification. This is what was in my hand when Tyler had me in a tentacle choke hold."

"Oh. I'm sorry. I guess I didn't realize that what you were holding was a new one. I thought it was still the old one."

"Where did it go?" Abby wades over to the spot by the window where Tyler held her hostage, kicking around some debris from his thrashing fits.

"Just try singing. Maybe it'll answer," Byron suggests.

"Yes, right." Rubbing the bruises on her neck, she tries to clear her throat. "Hold on a sec."

"We don't have a sec," Byron says, peering back out the window. More screams fill the air as residents stir and shuffle outside.

Abby hums through a gritty larynx. The wordless song is scratchy and deep. The tune makes a melody distinguishable from the screams and chatter outside, triggering the translucent turquoise cube to rise from the rubble, spinning slowly with a pleasant blue light.

The whirring gadget entrances Ben, the blue light reflecting in his dark irises. Blue beams pour from the cube's center, spinning in circles around the room. They continue to search, lost, just as they were in Byron's lab. Metaxysm gives one final energy pulse and fizzles out, falling back to the floor in a puff of dust.

"Why didn't that work?" Abby asks Byron, stunned.

Byron shrugs. "Nice song, though."

"Tyler's head is pulp. Maybe it didn't work because he's already dead?" Ben offers.

"Can we try the Knitting Sphere on him?" Abby asks.

Ben looks at Tyler's meaty face. "Uh...I don't think so."

Abby has already put the sphere in Tyler's cold hand, pumping it up and down. After several minutes, nothing happens.

"I don't think it can bring people back to life." Ben sighs, looking back at the shattered window where Jon went soaring.

"We probably need to get out of here before we're blamed for their deaths." Byron looks out the window. More screams and chatter swell, with an undercurrent of yipping dogs.

"We need to check the guest room first," Ben says.

"Right." Byron trots to the door, then peers around the corner and disappears into the hall.

Abby swipes Metaxysm from the floor and jams it back into her pocket before following Ben and Byron to the guest room. They halt at the closed door, Abby nearly bumping into Ben to see stagnant black ooze puddled in front of it. The edges have started to dry and crust over.

"It seems quiet in there," Abby says.

Ben puts an ear to the door and his good hand on the handle. Turning it slowly, he creaks the door open to get a good look at the nest. The door resists. He slams his dead arm into the door to open it wide. A pile of lifeless creatures lies at the foot of the door, causing resistance.

"Oh, thank God they're all dead." Abby puts a hand to her chest, "Wait, isn't that my gun?" She points at Ben as he slides it back under his waistband. Abby shrugs and puts Knitting Sphere in her pocket.

"Guys, we really need to get out of here," Byron says.

They make their way through the mucus-coated apartment out the door. Fresh air washes over them as they try to casually make their way to the parking lot without drawing attention from the screaming elders. Ben holds his arm, covering the bloodstained fabric.

"I'll take you home," Ben says, motioning Abby to his car. She shuffles to the passenger side and opens the door.

"Go ahead and get in. I'll be there in a sec," he says.

Ben looks around and checks the side door of Jon's car. He left it unlocked. Leaning inside, Ben chucks open the side console, riffling through the junk and feeling the plastic card-shaped badge. He rips it from the console to see Jon's healthy picture and name typed underneath. He pockets the badge and returns to his car, Abby waiting patiently for a ride.

Byron and Ben pull out of the circular drive, passing several police units peeling down Ashcroft and heading toward Circle Point. Abby closes her eyes, rehearsing every scenario she'll inevitably need to give to Soto for her involvement in the deaths of Jon and Tony.

INVESTIGATOR: EPILOGUE

"So TELL US, HOW did you come up with such a great idea? And did you know how much of an effect it would have on the world?" The brunette news host sits across from a dark man with a long button-up and limp left arm. He looks down, cracking a smile at the corner of his mouth.

"It was really just dumb luck, if I'm to be completely honest."

"Well, we can all certainly say your dumb luck has revolutionized health care as we know it!" The reporter and Ben laugh together as if they've rehearsed this conversation.

"Yes, it is indeed out of this world. It doesn't come without its limitations, though." Ben gestures at his limp arm.

"Please explain again how this happened."

"Well, I can't go into great detail Sue, but I was bitten and poisoned. Once the poison touched my muscle, it was damaged beyond repair."

Ben smiles at the thought of the poison damaging the arm enough to take away the random twitch.

Sue leans forward slightly. "But you tried testing the device on yourself, right? I mean, you know for sure that the effects are permanent?"

"Yes, I know for sure." Ben titters. "I even tried to set the dial to ninety-nine, but all I got was younger, less wrinkled, and tanned skin on one arm."

Sue laughs, her dark-plum lipstick smearing over her front teeth. "You have a colleague who goes on charity missions with the box, is that correct?"

Ben nods. "Mm, yes. Byron Todd."

"From what I understand, you have another coworker who researches all the little nuances of this gadget. So she'll be working on the box as well?"

"Ah, yes she will..."

Sue leans forward farther still, her voice deep and serious.

"And maybe she'll discover the key to aging in that invention?"

Ben looks down with a smile and a nod. "Perhaps, Sue. Perhaps she will."

Soto spared no expense in patching the hole Tyler made in the glass while also creating a new annex expansion. Abby strolls through the corridor of the annex, holding a gray hardcover notebook and the butt end of a black ballpoint pressed to her lips. Her wavy chestnut hair is pulled up to the top of her head, with wispy tendrils falling over the back of her neck. Her soles continue to tap through the corridor before she pauses to scribble down a few notes.

She hears a few Friday afternoon stragglers making their way through the atrium to the exit.

"Man, I think that chick gave me something..."

Abby turns to see a slender man with freckles strutting with a mousy redhead through the hall. Freckles reaches down to give his balls a quick scratch before disappearing through the front door.

Tucking the pen behind her ear, she turns and strides to the end of the hall, where a white door awaits. She badges through the door and plunks down into the office chair, facing a wide window overlooking dense pines and a fountained courtyard. She smiles as the outside light glows over her face.

"Good afternoon, Abigail Prince. It's now four o'clock." The Mag 10 monitor buzzes as the smooth male voice announces her reminder.

"Thanks, Frankie," she says, typing in a few notes and rocking back and forth in her chair. Her phone rings.

"Hey, Mom. What's up?"

"Just wanted to see how you're doing. It's been about a week since we last talked."

Abby grins. "Yes, it's been a while. I'm just finishing up work, and I'll go home soon. Do you and Dad want to do something this weekend?

"Yes, that would be lovely. We want to let you know we're both so proud of you."

"Thanks. I couldn't have done any of it without my parents."

As she hangs up the phone, she hears the buzz of a text.

Ben 4:16 p.m.: Hey are you still at work?

Abby 4:16 p.m.: Yes, are you coming by?

Ben 4:17 p.m.: I'm pulling in now.

Abby 4:17 p.m.: Okay, see you in a sec.

Abby looks at her desk. On top of the glossy glass surface is a palm-size gadget that looks like a green banana. She runs a finger over it, feeling the craftsmanship Jon had hammered into it.

She picks up the lemon-yellow-and-green Traquotori University mug from the warmer plate and swirls around an inch of settled coffee. As she takes a small sip, her nose scrunches at the old bitterness, so she flicks the plate off.

There's a knock at her door.

Abby turns to see Ben's wide grin through the window.

"Hey, I liked your interview," she tells him, letting him inside and pulling up a chair.

"I thought it went well!"

"So how does it feel to beat out Graviton?" She raises an eyebrow.

"I mean...technically...Tony did. But I had the idea too, so I guess it feels pretty good! I'm glad Jon's badge was a master key so I could get into Tony's lab."

"Where's the device now?"

"The Jewel Box? It's with Byron upstate. He's a busy man."

"I still think that's a silly name." Abby chuckles.

"Yeah, well, I'm an inventor, not a namer. Besides, Tony hadn't named it yet, and I couldn't call it the Knitting *Sphere*, now could I?"

Abby raises her arms and clicks her tongue.

"So, did you ever figure out what Jon's banana does?"

She turns to look at it, pinching its sides and running another finger along the curve. "Not yet, but I'll get there, I'm sure."

Ben sits for a moment, staring at Jon's banana and looking around the office. "Hey, can I see the museum again?"

"Really?" Abby rears back. "It's boring stuff."

"No way! I want to see all of it."

Smiling, she slides open a slender top drawer and pulls out a small silver key. "Okay, let's go, then."

They walk to the back of Abby's office. Once there, they stop at another white door, locked with no window and a two-tiered bronze plaque that says:

MUSEUM OF MYSTERIES: ABIGAIL
PRINCE, INVESTIGATOR.

"I still can't believe it, Abs."

She grins wordlessly as she unlocks the door, and the hinges creak open.

Automatic lights flicker on as they pass through the entry. Many shelves line the walls, containing all types of gadgets. Some sit bare on the shelf, while others are propped up on pedestals. A pegboard is mounted just inside, with a rainbow of colored metal panels swaying in the breeze of the HVAC.

It's all in the metal. Byron's words remind her of her mission, and she flicks a blue panel to hear it ring out.

"Are you any closer to unlocking any of those?" Ben asks, nodding at the ringing metal.

"Oh, yes, it's fascinating."

"What are Soto's rules about nondisclosure?" He hints for her to spill her secrets.

"I'll let you know in time. Right now, there are several things I don't know, and I want to make sure I'm not saying anything wrong."

"I understand." Ben grins and continues walking through the museum.

"This cluster belongs to Jon." She points to a row of several shelves lining the entirety of the wall, stacked over one another with multiple colors of curiosities in various shapes and sizes resting on each.

"Some of these are kinda dumb but could be improved with the right panel. When you have time, do you want me to show you?"

"Heck yeah!" Ben balls up his good fist in celebration while the other half of his body remains slack.

Abby moves down the museum with Ben next to her.

"And these were all of Byron's—"

Ben cuts her off. "I'd forgotten how many of these he had! You said he came to work on the weekends, too? Wow, that's dedication."

"Well, don't get too excited. A lot of these are lame." Abby laughs, thinking about that fateful Sunday when she ran into Byron and was subsequently kidnapped by Tyler. Byron's shelves had long lost room for all his gadgets. Once the shelves had been stuffed, Abby had piled more gadgets on the floor, verifying beforehand that it was safe to do so. Byron's section looks out of place against the others, with so much color and creativity stacked there.

The pair continue to walk past shelf after shelf of miscellaneous gadgets that have been explored and experimented on. Ben pokes at the little red orb sitting on one of his display shelves.

"I had no idea this thing only had a finite number of charges. If I'd known, I wouldn't have tried to test it as much as I did before showing it to you that one day." The orb is set into an intricately carved wooden plinth with a small silver nameplate embossed with the title: KNITTING SPHERE.

"I'm glad it still had a charge left it in for Byron." Abby smiles.

"Yeah...definitely."

Ben strolls through the museum more before stopping in front of a small cluster of items on a single shelf. All the items were crafted only in either black or white—Tony's shelf. Once the news broke that most of the gadgets Tony had created belonged to Byron, Soto sorted out everything he had claimed and assigned the patents to the proper owner. This shelf in the museum represents only Tony's actual accomplishments, none of them patented.

Ben stares at the handful of items on Tony's shelf for a long minute before returning to Abby. "I wonder why he only created in black and white?"

Abby shrugs. "Maybe he couldn't think 'outside the box'?"

"Ha. Ha. Very funny—outside the box," Ben says back in a mocking laugh.

They both knew Tony lucked out with the Jewel Box, creating it after combing through Ben's research notes using the bug in his computer and one of the only two panels he knew how to use.

"Honestly, though," Abby says, "I felt a little bad for him... I mean, his father is the CEO of Soto Labs. He probably was trying to live up to him or impress him however he could."

"By stabbing everyone else in the back," Ben adds, wagging a finger.

Abby shrugs. Ben looks at her, raising a corner of his mouth as if chewing the inside of his cheek.

"Hey, I'm sorry about Tyler," he says.

Abby looks down at her feet. "Ah, it's okay. I mean, I feel bad about him for sure, but after everything, there wasn't really anything we could do. I'm kinda thankful for his death, to be honest..."

Ben raises an eyebrow, parting his mouth in surprise. "What do you mean by that?"

"Well, if it weren't for him, we probably would have been blamed for the deaths of Jon and Tony. No, scratch that—I would have been blamed."

Abby takes small steps toward the back of the museum. A vertical line of shelves decorates the back wall, with a display light cast over them. Ben follows without argument, knowing the truth of her words.

The center shelf has a small bell jar displayed over a wooden plate, with Metaxysm resting flat on the wooden surface, mesmerizing with its turquoise color. Several small cracks spiderweb over the surface of the jar. Abby runs a finger over some of the webbing.

"I need to replace this bell jar soon," she says, rubbing her index finger over her thumb, tiny cuts from the glass welling up on the pad of her finger.

"Is it vibrating still?"

"Sort of... It's still humming in there. I guess the glass can only take it for so long. Maybe I should just put a plastic bell over it instead." She sticks her red index finger in her mouth.

Metaxysm has an embossed silver nameplate as well. It rests between two closed jars filled with murky off-yellow fluid labeled "Spawn 1" and "Spawn 2." Ben pokes the jar labeled "Spawn 1," and the little black creature inside jiggles, suspended in the fluid. It then bobs in the suspension, dead as the day they left Tyler's apartment. The murky liquid casts a sickening glow under the spotlight above the shelves. Spawn 2 holds one of the older creatures in a larger jar. The fluid is darker, with bubbles foaming on the surface.

"I still feel bad, though," Ben continues, "I know you kinda liked him."

Abby sighs, thinking back to Tyler's handsome face and crystalline eyes. "Yeah, a little. Until... well, you know."

She brings her face down one shelf under Metaxysm to an even larger jar. The fluid inside isn't quite as murky, but it isn't clear either. Ash blond hair floats in the liquid, and the eyes are rolled back into the skull, showing only red and oozing capillaries through alabaster jellied whites. The crooked nose sticks out over a row of mangled teeth, and a long tongue dangles down through the liquid to touch the bottom of the jar.

The little silver tag reads: Tyler Rowe, Senior Accountant.

***

[Return to chapter "Disturbed"] (Page 146)

Paralysis

Ben has chosen to activate Metaxysm

RATHER THAN RISK MAKING a false move, Ben stands still, gun pointed at Tyler. His eyes dart between Metaxysm resting in Abby's palm and Tyler's inhuman gaze. Tyler looks at Abby when she makes a tiny squeak. His scaly neck buzzes as his black eyes pore over every inch of her in his grip. He unhinges his jaw, emitting another primal scream. Ben squeezes his eyes shut, trying not to make a sound. Any sudden move might send him to lie next to Tony or Jon.

"Sing to the gadget," Byron hisses at Ben. "Sing to it!"

The ethereal hum of the object fills Ben's ears, putting him in a trance. He has a moment of clarity and closes his eyes. Slowly, he sings the first song that comes to his mind.

"Little Shane, little Shane boy from the stars," he starts. Tyler roars, jarring Abby and shaking her open hand. The cube rattles perilously in her palm.

"...tried to catch Venus but landed on Maaaaars," not remembering the tune to his boyhood song, he sings it to the tune of "Twinkle, Twinkle, Little Star".

Little Shane, little Shane boy from the staaaarrrs, tried to catch Venus but landed on Maaaars. His melody ignites something in Metaxysm 2.0, causing it to elevate from Abby's palm and bob in the air.

Byron looks at Ben from the corner of his eye and tries to sing the song with Ben, reading his lips for cues on the lyrics.

"Little Shane, little Shane," Byron sings in his deep voice.

"...boy from the stars," Ben continues.

"Tried to catch Venus and landed on Mars!" they sing in unison, causing Metaxysm 2.0 to light up while spinning aloft.

Tyler lets out another bloodcurdling scream, crouching back on thick haunches made of alien meat. Ben opens his eyes to see the tentacle holding Abby's throat, loosening and pushing her violently to the side. She hits the wall, leaving a dent in the drywall, which bursts open, spraying a dust cloud around her. Metaxysm 2.0 stays afloat, hovering near Tyler, emitting a soft blue glow. The inner light pierces through, spraying light beams onto Tyler's grotesque form.

In the corner, Abby coughs hard, gasping in new breaths as she's finally free from Tyler's grasp. She springs upright, brushing the drywall off her pants and facing Tyler. Rather than hum, she sings softly. The lyrics to "Every Little Thing She Does Is Magic" fall from her lips, although deep and hoarse. She closes her eyes and remembers Lee, a solitary tear clinging to her bottom eyelash. Tyler freezes, transfixed by the melody coming. His blackened eyes roll toward Abby; her voice is what's needed to send the creature back to hell.

Metaxysm spins faster, the light now burning into the tentacles. Silver wisps of smoke rise from the pulsing mass, creating an acrid aroma of burning rubber and tar. Tyler's neck scales rattle quickly as he stares with milky, bloody eyes at the blue glow dancing and burning the flesh he has grown to love. He emits one more scream and charges at Ben.

Byron leaps forward in front of Ben, knocking him over and landing on top of him while the charred and inflamed tentacles slap and pound the floor and walls. Byron grunts and coughs hard, blood spattering from his mouth. Ben feels the warmth of Byron's blood soaking into his jeans as he remains pinned underneath the large square of a man.

As Abby continues her tune, the rotating beams of blue glow puncture the air and pulsate, concentrating thick rays on the thrashing tentacles. The smoke intensifies, drying out Abby's vocals and causing her to choke. The short song she gave it is enough to continually power the cube, which is hovering on its own and continuing to sear Tyler. While the light spreads over the tentacles, they slow down and freeze as if turning to stone. The movement reminds Ben of the poison frozen in his left arm.

The gray meat, a once glossy and mucus-covered surface, morphs into dull, lifeless ash under the heat of Metaxysm's lasers. The ash bursts and dissipates, no longer supporting the beast. Tyler's human form totters and thumps to the floor. His naked body lies still, draped halfway over Byron's limp torso. Ben writhes under both bodies, attempting to slide out from under them.

"Guys..." Byron coughs out, spitting out another mouthful of blood, "Are you okay?" His voice is weak.

Abby hurries to him and kneels on the floor beside him. "Yes, Byron. We're okay. Save your strength. We'll get you help, don't worry." Her bloodshot eyes struggle for moisture as she tends to him, frantically placing her hands on his stomach in an attempt to squish his intestines back into his body. Ben pats Byron from underneath.

She uses the strength of her legs to kick Tyler's limp body off Byron. Her hands shake as she pulls Byron's arms up to free Ben from underneath. Once released, Ben crouches beside Abby, trying to make sense of Byron's wound.

"The cops will be here soon for sure," Abby croaks. "Someone will find Jon out there any minute now."

"You saved my life," Ben tells Byron.

Byron grins wide and red, lifting his head to look at the wound. His weakened muscles fight for a drop of strength. He grunts and drops his head back to the floor.

Abby's lip trembles as she looks at her dying friend. Sadness flips to rage when she looks at Tyler's body, still warm and half draped over Byron. She grunts and kicks Tyler hard enough that he rolls over and thuds to the floor. The handsome, dusty-blond-haired man who had begun to scratch her itch for companionship has transformed into a nightmare. His teeth are coated in black blood, which trickles from the corners of his mouth. Various wet and deep red holes dot his body where the alien appendages sprouted. She averts her eyes to avoid Tyler's nakedness.

"Can someone please... Help me with this...knife?" Byron lifts his head a tiny bit, fat fingers feeling around at the handle of Ben's knife sticking out of his gut.

Ben reaches down and looks Byron dead in the eye. "This is going to hurt." Still looking at Byron for approval, he wraps his fingers around the handle.

Byron nods at him and closes his eyes. Ben tugs at the handle gently, causing the large man to groan. He stops and looks down at his belt. After unbuckling the fake leather wrap and folding it up, he presses the folds to Byron's lips. Byron accepts the gift without opening his eyes, clamping down hard on the pleather with bloodied teeth.

Ben steadies his grip again, pulling out the blade. The serrated edge pulls at the opening, tearing apart fresh wounds as it cuts its way back out of the hole. Byron screams, his throat digging farther into the belt. Once the blade is free, a squirt of blood pulses from the wound. His heartbeat pounds hard, then slows as he lies face-up, gurgling.

Ben frantically looks around. Tony's corpse lies crumpled in a corner, no longer plagued by competition. The hole in the shattered window that lets in the warm breeze holds the impetus of Jon's demise and the broken body lying on the red sidewalk below. Abby's lip quivers with fresh tears carve over dusty cheeks.

"If only we had Tony's stupid gadget..." Her voice quivers as she sits beside Byron, placing her small hand into his.

Ben jerks his head up and pats his pocket. "I brought Knitting Sphere!" he says, jamming his hand into his pocket again, pulling out the unremarkable small red orb and holding it out to her.

Abby swipes the sphere, smashes the little button, and crams it into Byron's palm, folding his fingers over it and holding it in place with her own hands. *You shouldn't bring a prototype outside the lab*, Ben's chastisement echoes in her mind. She's grateful he didn't take his own advice.

"Please work, please work," she chants.

Abby places her forehead on Byron's beefy fist. While she weeps and repeats her mantra, the familiar warmth spreads over her brow from Byron's fingers. She rears back to see the same biological glow, showcasing red vessels and bones. The effects travel up through Byron's arm, waking him from his pain. The trio watches as the light travels through his body until it settles around the wet opening that splits his belly button in two. The brightness intensifies, illuminating the edges of torn flesh and sending pinholes of light from capillaries.

Byron cries out an animalistic howl. Ben and Abby watch as the blood that sprayed from the wound creates a reverse fountain of red back into his body. A small portion of his small intestine that had been poking out of the wound jolts to life, then slithers back inside his body, causing the big man to emit another low groan.

"What are you doing to me?" he yells at the pair, who have been patiently watching the gruesome reversal. They say nothing to him.

Byron wails again when the flesh around the wound moves on its own accord as if a thousand maggots are squirming under the surface. It then begins to glue itself back together.

The sphere completes its job, finalizing the reversal as the glow dims. The wound closes up entirely as if it had never existed, only evidenced by the hole that remains in his shirt.

Byron jolts upright, looking at the hole and the pale pink flesh underneath. After handing the sphere back to Ben, he fumbles around with the fabric, feeling around at the unblemished skin in shock.

"Was that *your* gadget?" he asks Ben.

"Yeah, an idea Tony stole." Ben looks back at Tony's lifeless form. *He's clearly dead. There's no way to save him with this.*

"Well, I'll be damned. That was just as painful as getting stabbed," Byron laughs.

Abby can't peel her eyes off Tony. She suddenly feels sad for him despite how awful he was in life.

"Is it over?" Ben, sitting on the floor, looks at Tyler's limp body, riddled with meaty holes and dusted with remnants of tentacle ash.

Byron grunts as he rolls to his side to get up. He limps over debris to look out the window. Jon's body lies on the pavement, sides split in two. An older woman in slippers and night attire walks her little terrier with a pink leash and bells on the collar. She shuffles curiously toward Jon's body and lets out a bloodcurdling wail.

"Cops will definitely be here soon now," he says.

A weak groan comes from Tyler's mangled body. He rolls to the side, looking down at the floor. Ben takes a sharp step back.

"W-what is going on...?" Tyler's weak voice wavers.

Abby kneels next to Tyler and moves his face to look at hers.

"What is going on? Why can't I move?" he says

She sees several holes in his body and points at Ben. "Give him the Knitting Sphere."

He puts the little orb in Abby's hand, and she transfers the gadget to Tyler. Activating the button does nothing.

"Why is this not working?" Abby clutches Tyler's fist and shakes it up and down in a feeble attempt to make the healing powers boot up and start their work. Tyler groans and rolls his head to the side.

"We used it on Byron. Maybe it needs to recharge? Oh, and I also used it on myself when one of those creatures bit my hand." Ben points at his limp arm.

Abby's eyes go wide, and she sucks in a sharp breath. "The creatures!" She drops Tyler's hand and runs to the guest bedroom with Ben tailing her.

She halts at the closed door, stagnant black ooze puddled in front of it. The edges have started to dry and crust over.

"It seems quiet in there," Abby says.

Ben puts an ear to the door and his good hand on the handle. Turning it slowly, he creaks the door open to get a good look at the nest. The door resists. He slams his dead arm into the door to open it wide. A pile of lifeless creatures lies at the foot of the door, which was the source of the resistance.

"Oh, thank God they're all dead." Abby puts a hand to her chest, "Wait. Isn't that my gun?"

She points at Ben as he slides it back under his waistband. He smiles and shrugs.

"I'm going to call 911," Byron states.

Abby jogs over to what remains of the bed and pulls the sheet off. She drapes it over Tyler's body, leaving his head to poke out.

"Hello, I need to report..." Byron's voice echoes in the background.

"I'm so confused," Tyler croaks.

"Shh, it's okay. We'll talk later. Right now, you're badly injured."

Abby, Ben, and Byron stand side by side in the parking lot of Soto Labs. The Monday sun crests from the horizon, illuminating the building and casting a long shadow over the trio.

"Tyler will be fine," Byron reassures Abby.

She nods, staring pensively at the building. She knows her time is up at Soto. No one could possibly create an instrument of destruction like that and keep their job.

Scaffolding surrounds the building as workers have already begun restructuring the holes Tyler burst through while adding a new annex.

"It was fun while it lasted." Abby lets out a sigh, deep and scratchy, as she rubs her injured throat.

"Don't talk like that. You never know what's going to happen."

"Well, Jon and Tony are dead, and ultimately it's my fault. Tony was the CEO's son—he won't want me around."

"You might get a patent?" Ben lifts an eyebrow and tilts an ear to his shoulder.

"I honestly don't care about that."

"Where is Metaxysm now?" Byron asks.

"In my pocket, ready to turn over to Soto. Hopefully for destruction."

THREE WEEKS HAVE PASSED since the showdown at Circle Point. Now the downtown buzzes with distracted pedestrians traveling to and from work, from home to restaurants, hailing cabs… Life carries on as if nothing happened that fateful night at Tyler's apartment. Abby walks among the crowd toward Memorial Mercy West, Tyler's new home for a while. She carries a bundle of white daisies in a show of friendship and surrender.

"Friend or family?" the receptionist asks once Abby tells her Tyler's name.

"Friend." Abby's voice is still deep and scratchy.

"Fifth floor. The nurses' station is right outside the elevator to the left."

"Thanks."

Abby makes her way to the fifth floor, weaving past oblivious people. An older man in slippers shuffles along the stained carpet, pushing an IV cart. The backside of his gown is tied loosely and threatening to open.

"You're doing great!" The old man's nurse cheers him along, holding his elbow.

Abby smiles and gets Tyler's room number from the nurses' station. She clutches the daisies in one hand; with her other, she feels her neck from the bruising he gave her. The past few weeks have been kind to her healing process, transforming the purple and black welts across her skin into a blooming yellowish shadow. The only evidence of her trauma is her altered voice.

Tyler's healing, she knew, would be a trial unlike anything that someone like him had ever experienced. This is the second day he's been awake from his medically induced coma. She approaches his room. The door is open, and she hears faint voices inside. She peers into the room. The curtain is pulled shut, and light filters through the window, casting Tyler's shadow against it and the shadow of someone else standing there, talking to him. The room is light and cheery—a welcome sight from the last time she saw him. Vases of brightly colored roses arranged with baby's breath and get-well cards line the small table across from his bed. She looks down at her pitiful daisies and sighs.

She raps lightly on the frame, and the person standing whips the curtain aside. The woman gives Abby a sad smile and turns back to Tyler.

"You have a friend," she says, opening the curtain wide.

Tyler is lying on his stomach, arms draped to the side with the bed bent at a queer angle to support his back. Several machines monitor his vitals.

He turns his head from the window to look at Abby. "Oh hey," he says, his tone suggestive of a man defeated.

"Hey." She takes a small step forward, "I brought these for you." She holds the daisies in front of her like a kid at show-and-tell.

Tyler smiles, deep bruising surrounding his eye sockets. Abby sees red streaks along his neck where those accursed scales have healed over.

"Hey, Mom, can you let me and Abby talk alone?" Tyler says. The woman's hair is the same shade as her son's: dusty blond with a light strawberry highlight.

"Sure, hon. I'll go downstairs for a bit and try to find your sister. I think she's on shift today. Just let me know when you want me back." She walks past Abby, her eyes are the same crystalline color as her son's. He favors her well.

Once Tyler's mother leaves the room, Abby holds out the daisies toward the table of roses and looks at Tyler for approval. He nods.

"Your sister works here?" she asks.

"Yeah, she's one of the nurses in the NICU. Doesn't really jibe with my situation."

"How are you feeling?" she asks, trying to lay the bouquet across the table where they can be seen.

"I've been better," he japes.

"Yeah... How bad is it?"

Abby knows full well how nasty Tyler's wounds are, having been with him when Metaxysm evaporated his extra limbs, leaving deep holes in his back and blisters for skin.

"Well, I'll never walk again," he says. "The holes in my back went down to the bone in some places. I'm officially paralyzed from the neck down."

Abby cringes at the thought, feeling a shock of sympathetic pain in her own spine. "Geez" is all she can muster at the moment.

"Every once in a while, the nurse flips me, but right now, I can't stay on my back for long."

Abby sees the thin bedsheet clinging to his rear, swallowed by his crack. Being paralyzed, Tyler can't feel it, let alone do anything about it. Abby walks over and pulls the sheet taut, then pats him on the shoulder.

"I'm sorry, Tyler."

He pauses for a moment. "I would tell you that 'it's okay,' but I'd be lying. Thanks for your sympathy, though."

"What's going to happen now?"

He blows a long puff of air through pursed lips. "I dunno. I have to focus on getting better first. Then I can figure it out. How are things at Soto?"

"I don't know anymore."

"What do you mean?" His head jerks as if trying to lift his limp body to face her.

"Oh... they fired me."

"They what?"

"Yeah, I guess I just wasn't cutting it there." *And they blamed Tony and Jon's deaths on me.*

The side of Tyler's face sinks into his pillow. "What's your plan now, then?"

"I don't know. Maybe I'll put science aside. Maybe I'll write a book?"

"Ha! You could write about what could have happened if you hadn't saved me with your gadget."

Abby's smile is tainted with guilt, knowing it was her gadget that set Tyler on that course to begin with. "It's wild how the world doesn't know what happened in your apartment."

"Right? So much damage..."

"I bet your landlord was *thrilled*," she says, laughing.

"He probably didn't even see it, honestly. The minions from Soto went there to cover it up. Strange organization, I say. How's your neck?"

Abby runs her fingers across the sides of her neck. "I'll be fine."

"Your voice is deeper..."

"Just a little."

Tyler snorts. "Did anyone find any of those weird little things I made?"

"Maybe. But they were dead." She gazes out the window. "Once I activated Metaxysm, your tentacles turned to ash, causing the creatures to die. But if Soto covered everything up, they probably took those little beasties too."

Tyler sinks into the pillow again. "Hmmm."

"Hey, Tyler?"

"Hm?" His eyes droop with exhaustion.

"Do you remember anything?"

He pauses, looking at her from the corner of his eye. The crystalline iris digs deep into his temple.

"Yes. Everything."

At that moment, two nurses stride toward Tyler. Abby scoots over as each nurse chooses a side of his bed. Carefully, they scoop their hands under his abdomen, working in unison to turn him over to his back.

"We'll be back in a few," one of them gruffly tells Tyler, who nods.

The two nurses shuffle out of the room as if Abby isn't even there. She looks at her feet, thinking about everything that happened while

Tyler wasn't in control. The fact that he can remember everything is a sore spot she isn't sure she is ready to prod into, but a selfish side of her wants confirmation that he's guilty. He knows her gadget saved him, but does he know it also destroyed him?

"I'm sorry," she says, "that you remember everything."

Tyler stares at her, unable to move and barely blinking. His neck is scrunched back against his pillow, making his chin double and nose appear more crooked.

"I should apologize to *you*." He labors to talk at the angle his nurses put him in. "I was inside my body, but I had no control. It was like...it was like trying to scream from the bottom of the ocean. I wanted to stop hurting you, but...I had no control. *None*."

Abby looks down and nods. Any attraction she's ever felt for Tyler is gone. That fact isn't his fault—it's hers. She bites her lip and wrinkles her nose to stay the burning tears in her eyes. She looks at her watch, not wanting to be around for the next bed flip.

"Well, goodbye, Tyler."

He opens his mouth to say something but stops and nods at her.

Abby turns and leaves, passing his mom in the hallway. She doesn't see Abby, and Abby isn't about to say anything to her.

Tyler remembers.

She reconsiders finalizing her goodbye to him. If he remembers everything, maybe he can exonerate her. Or better yet, praise her for saving him? *Do I want to go back to Soto?*

Her phone buzzes as she walks through the parking lot.

Ben 12:26 p.m.: Hey, we miss you over here.

Abby 12:27 p.m.: Aw, I miss you guys too.

Ben 12:29 p.m.: The new apprentice isn't nearly as likable as you. Very arrogant.

Abby 12:30 p.m.: Really? That sucks! I'm sorry!

Ben 12:31 p.m.: Yeah, hopefully she doesn't turn into another Tony.

Abby 12:31 p.m.: Guard your ideas!

Ben 12:33 p.m.: Right? What are you doing this weekend? Byron and I were thinking about catching a movie or doing something else. We don't know what yet.

Abby 12:34 p.m.: Yeah, that sounds like fun!

Ben 12:24 p.m.: Awesome, I'll let you know the details later.

Abby 12:36 p.m.: Sounds like a plan! By the way...Tyler remembers everything.

***

Mulligan! [Return to chapter "Disturbed"] (Page 146)

Paralysis

creeps

Ben has chosen to rush Tyler

THE HARDENED SCALES ON Tyler's neck quake as he looks at Ben with milky, bloody eyes. He emits one more scream and further tightens his grip around Abby's neck.

Ben doesn't move. He raises the gun in line with the yellowed human head perched on the beast. He squints an eye, watching the large boils over the surface of the human skin shrink and swell as if breathing. *Maybe if I hit one of those...*

"Dhokn't," Abby chokes out her disapproval, trying to shake her head simultaneously.

Ben points the gun back at Tyler's face. A high-pitched wail screeches through the air, scales clacking. Abby squeezes her eyes shut as Byron crushes his ear against his shoulder. The scream vibrates like wild drums in Ben's ears.

Click.

Tyler's rage ignites. He pounds his appendages over the floor, through the walls, and raking over shelves. Knickknacks shatter across the hard floor, striking Ben's foot. He ducks as a large book comes sweeping at his head, smacking the wall behind him. A swollen droplet of sweat trickles over Byron's temple. His view darts back and forth between man, woman, and monster. His muscles tighten in a low crouch as he waits for his cue to spring. Ben slaps the gun against his leg, hoping to knock it back into order.

Click. Click.

Damn.

Ben chucks the gun aside, and it skitters across the hard floor before coming to a stop with a thump at the baseboard. He closes his eyes, attempting to match Tyler's rage. *This is a pissing match now.*

Ben stands defiant. He squares his shoulders, arcing his hands behind him in a challenge. He screams at Tyler, pulling a fearsome din from the bottom of his gut to create a guttural demonic yawl. Abby's eyes widen. He charges.

Tyler's neck scales rattle at the incoming rush. The muscular mass flicks Ben like a gnat, and he flies across the room, crashing into the wall beside Byron. Before Ben can blink, Tyler curls Abby against his chest and leaps out the shattered window, crushing Jon farther into the pavement. The sound of grinding bones reverberates through the window.

Ben's chin drapes over his chest, eyes closed, his body covered in bits of drywall. Byron leaps toward the broken window, watching Tyler's shadow stretch and disappear into the pines, using both legs and tentacles to race through the night and out of sight, Abby in tow. He turns to Ben, who's still unconscious against the wall.

Byron rakes fat fingers through his hair, gripping the strands tight and pulling. Remembering the guest room, he heads to the door. The black pool is drying, leaving a crackled edge. He bursts into the room, splintering the jamb to find only a pile of dead black creatures—some that exploded on the door and walls and others that suffocated under the mass piled up against the door.

After standing there for a few moments until satisfied that nothing is moving, Byron returns to the main bedroom. Ben is still slumped against the wall. Byron trots to the open window, looking around—for what, he's unsure. Jon's body lies on the pavement, sides split in two. An older woman in slippers and night attire walks her little terrier with a pink leash and bells on the collar. She shuffles curiously toward Jon's body and lets out a bloodcurdling wail.

"Ben, Ben! Get up!" He jostles Ben's shoulders. His head flops back and forth. "Come on, dude! Ben!"

A few more shakes and Ben's eyes flutter open. He draws in a sharp breath and puts a hand to his head. The screaming outside echoes through the bedroom.

"Should we go after them?" Byron asks.

"Go after who?"

"Tyler and Abby! Snap out of it, Ben—we need to get out of here!"

Ben shakes his head again, wiping a dirty hand down the length of his face, rubbing his skin pink.

Byron's eyes light up, and he moves back to the open window, riffling through debris and throwing random items behind him.

"What are you doing?" Ben croaks.

Byron continues to shuffle through the debris. "Abby had another Metaxysm with her. You saw it, didn't you?"

"Yeah, I think so. I didn't know that was a new one."

"Sing something," Byron says.

"What? No. Why?"

"Fine, I will."

Byron sings "Twinkle, Twinkle, Little Star," hoping the gadget will rise from the debris and he can grab it. Ben rears back and scrunches his face.

"That's just awful," Ben holds his head in pain, mainly from the impact but partly from the screeching song.

Nothing happens.

Byron stops and slumps to the floor. "It's not here."

"Why were you singing?"

"Abby made a new version that could have turned everything around," Byron says. "She made it this morning, and we tested it. She told me about the first version... This one had a failsafe in it."

Ben gets up as gingerly as an old man rising from bed. He runs his good hand over his pants in a feeble attempt to brush crumbs of drywall off them.

"So what does singing—horribly singing—have anything to do with the new gadget?" Ben grimaces, blood staining his teeth. During his flight into the wall, he bit his tongue.

Byron relaxes his shoulder and sighs. He continues looking around the floor but can't find the little turquoise cube anywhere.

"Like I said, singing reverses the damage."

"You didn't say that. Why didn't you say that?"

"I didn't have a chance before you went all primal on him."

Ben holds his forehead and squeezes his eyes shut. More screams flow in through the window.

"Seriously, we need to get the hell out of here," Byron says, pulling on Ben's arm. Ben sluggishly complies.

What did I do wrong? Ben skids his shoes through the debris to follow Byron.

"We need to track them," Byron says.

They creep through the lot, trying not to be seen by the screaming, horrified residents.

"Hold on," Ben says. He walks over to Jon's car and tries the door. Fortunately, he left it unlocked. Leaning inside, he opens the center console and riffles around until his fingers wrap around the square plastic badge. Pulling it out, he sees Jon's photo with his name printed boldly underneath. Ben pockets the badge and heads back to Byron.

"Okay, how do you want to track them?"

creeps: epilogue

"ARE YOU OUT THERE?" a deep, gruff voice says into the radio. "If you are, follow the signal."

Byron clicks off the radio. He looks at Ben and shrugs. With a sigh, Ben scratches his beard, salt and pepper scattered throughout the wiry hairs.

"We've been holed up in here, trying to reach Abby, for six months. I don't think she's alive anymore." Byron rakes fat, dirty fingers through long, greasy hair. Ben ignores him.

Months prior, Byron and Ben had found themselves back at Soto Labs after a weak attempt at trailing Tyler. Like good hunters, they'd followed cracked branches, looked for subtle signs of activity, and watched for large globs of slime. After a long, hot day of tracking, they realized they had followed Tyler's original trail to find Abby at Soto. The whole day was lost, and by the time they'd reached Soto, black spawn had already begun tracking *them*. The only place they knew to secure themselves was in B6.

"She *may* be dead, son, but there are others out there who might find comfort in our voices and need a place to hide." Tyler's old neighbor, Charles, points casually at Byron, rocking back and forth on a ripped leather desk chair.

"What's comfort going to do?" Byron raises his hands in an exaggerated question.

"Can I say som'thin'?" a thin, wiry man around Ben's age swings his legs back and forth like a child over the edge of the tall central bench.

"Go for it." Byron raises his arms again and turns around.

"If it weren't for the radio, me and ol' Duane wouldn'ta found you guys."

"And what good did it do you, Jerry? We're all stuck in here, waiting for the next wave of slimy black piggies and running out of resources."

"Well, at least we're not on drugs anymore..." Jerry's voice trails off.

"Speaking of which, I need to charge up the worm." Ben heads to the break room and removes the dirty, worn section of false wall that hides the electrical panel. He flips four separate switches and then returns to the central area.

"Don't call it that," Byron chides him.

"Abby called it that."

"*Called*. Past tense."

"Guys, why don't we try calling out on the radio again?" Jerry pleads.

"Hold on." Ben holds up a finger, then runs to the front room and peers through the small window, looking into the steel corridor. The rings hum and shift just a bit before making sluggish rounds. He checks his watch, the cracked face forcing him to turn his wrist at different angles to catch the time. "It's two fifteen. They should be here any minute."

"Good. I'm ready to get some sleep." Charles yawns, fanning his hand over his gaping mouth.

"Not before cleaning up Bella's poop." Byron points to a corner.

"Oh, sorry. I didn't know she went over there." The little white dog sits proudly next to Charles, panting obediently by his side.

Duane breathes heavily, snoring occasionally on a makeshift bed in the middle of the floor.

Ben stands sentinel at the door, face pressed against the glass and leaving a plume of fog. Every once in a while, he wipes it with his sleeve, then resumes peering through the window. His left arm remains limp at his side, no longer wracked with nerve twitches from the piggy poison.

The door on the opposite side of the corridor is bolted tight—moonlight beams in through the crack at the bottom. Long ago, any light piercing this place would have been inconceivable. Crafty creatures, these piggies. They had found a way to burrow directly to this hiding spot. Byron theorizes that Tyler orders these waves. *But why only at this time? Why only at 2:23 a.m.?* Ben has always wondered. He looks at his watch again.

A few little shadows glide back and forth in front of the moonlit crack.

"They're here," Ben states, his voice deadened by the door.

"How's the, ah...*rings?*" Charles asks, trying to avoid provoking Byron's ire by calling them the worm despite finding it easier to say.

"They're turning but not fast enough yet. Soon, though."

More shadows appear. Ben cracks the door open slightly to listen. Weak thumping sounds rap at the outer door, while the shadows continue to glide and jerk. A little black tendril squeezes under the crack, methodically feeling the floor as if tasting its surface. More black tendrils unfurl and bounce up and down to taste the ground, looking to Ben like many squishy, rotten fingers playing the piano. He shuts the door and locks it once again.

"They're about to squeeze in," he says.

"The rings?"

"About there."

Jerry continues to swing his legs while yawning as Charles pats Bella's head, cooing at her. Byron stands by the radio, arms crossed and looking like a pissed-off brick house.

"Almost..." Ben's breath on the window has turned into drips of water.

In unison, all the black fingers retreat from under the door. Ben watches as a black bubble forms, squeezing and writhing from the crack. Then another...and another, until several little piggies with black button eyes and razor-sharp teeth begin slithering down the hallway of the worm.

"Babies again," Ben states, looking back at the crew. Charles yawns with Jerry while Byron remains stiff in the corner by the radio, glaring through bushy eyebrows.

"Let us know when they're all dead. I'm an old man," Charles says. Ben gives him a thumbs-up, his gaze still fixed on the worm.

The rings spin faster, almost as fast as they should. Dozens of the little black creatures melt into the room, squeezing from underneath the door to pop up on the other side. They slither and crawl over the floor toward the man watching them through the window. Little teeth gnash as the creatures pick up speed, wriggling through the worm. Eventually, they find Ben's door.

Ben looks down at the black demons with disgust. Night after night, these demon spawn visit them, giving them the day hours to hunt, scavenge...survive. There has been no hint of Abby in the last several months, and Ben has begun to lose hope of ever finding her. The increased in-fighting with Byron is tearing at his mind, making him lose patience and will.

"What did you do with Abby, you little pricks?" he mutters.

The creatures snap and snarl, building a ladder to meet Ben's face in the window.

"*What did you do with her?*" He slaps an open palm next to the window, spraying the glass with spit.

Duane stirs, turning to look at Ben. Charles's mouth is agape, and Byron remains still in the corner. Jerry's feet have stopped swinging.

Ben continues to slap the door, cursing the pile of demons as they hurl themselves against the other side of the door. Some of them explode, spraying thick, dark liquid over the hall. The rings reach velocity.

The floor begins to vibrate faintly. The pile of creatures shakes with the vibrations, tumbling from their tower and meandering drunkenly through the corridor. Ben watches them like he always does. They rise up and down on their slick little tentacles, swaying viciously back and forth.

A cacophony of squeals can be heard through the door, earning them their nickname of "piggies." The squealing reaches a crescendo until their soft bodies begin to pop, one after the other, spraying black goo across the walls, the door, and the floor. Once the last one pops, Ben cracks open the door and spits on the river of blood. He turns to the crew, who've been watching him throughout his angry outburst.

"I-I'm going to check the lifts." Jerry hops off the counter and grabs Jon's ID badge, sitting by Byron near the radio. Ben nods, wiping his mouth.

As he looks at the grump in the corner, Ben's heart softens at their memories. "Remember how we found the lifts?" he asks Byron.

"How could I forget that?" Byron grunts.

Ben chuckles, and then his smile becomes melancholy as he stares off momentarily.

"How *did* you find the lifts?" Charles has perked up from eavesdropping.

Ben shakes his head, twisting his mouth into another half-smile. "Ah, it was nothing, really. Before you came around, it was just me and By. We heard a banging noise coming from Abby's lab. We thought maybe it was her trying to find a way in or something—but it wasn't her."

Jerry comes out of Tony's lab and then badges into Ben's. Ben pauses to watch him.

"Who was it then?"

"The night elf," Ben says, chuckling.

"The what now?"

"It was the damn night stocker," Byron interrupts, unfolding his arms and fussing with the radio once again.

"The night *stalker*?"

"No, no." Ben shakes his head. "The guy who comes at night to stock the shelves. We—Abby and I—call him the night elf."

"*Called*. Past tense," Byron murmurs.

"Would you stop that?" Ben shoots a glare at the back of Byron's head.

"Ohhh, okay then," Charles replies, turning one eyebrow skyward.

Jerry emerges from Ben's lab to move to Abby's. Ben looks back to Charles.

"He was trapped in there. Apparently, he had no clue that the world was ending. Until he *became* aware..."

Charles opens his mouth to speak.

"Oh, crap!" Jerry's scream is muffled through Abby's lab door, followed by the sound of a viscous wet slap hitting the floor. Ben rushes to her lab door to peer through the window. He raps on it. Jerry's mouth is frozen open, eyes wide. He turns to Ben, the left half of his face and shoulder coated in black goo. He grimaces while picking up his feet high and walking along an imaginary tightrope toward Ben. He opens the door for him.

"Watch your step," he says as Ben strides inside.

The floor is coated with chunks of flesh and an ink-black pool. The lift remains lowered, more of the creatures' blood dripping from the sidebar. A pair of little legs dangle from the lift, slowly swaying.

"Were there no piggies in the other labs?" Ben asks.

"I've only checked yours and Tony's so far."

Ben clenches the muscles in his jaw. He surveys the lab and then spins toward the lift.

"I'm going to check outside," he says, returning to the central area to confer with Byron.

"Did you clean it?" Byron asks.

Ben loads the clip into the pistol Abby left behind. "I just cleaned it this morning. It shouldn't jam."

"Don't do anything stupid."

"Charles, Duane, I'll be going to investigate outside. Help Byron guard the worm door for any stragglers," Ben says to the men, who nod.

Ben heads back into Abby's lab and relays his intent to Jerry. The man nods and motions toward the lift, still coated in sludge.

"Give me the cue when you're ready to come back down...or bang wildly if you're in trouble," he says, thumb poised over a small button set into the wall.

Ben rises via the lift, encircled by smaller rotating rings, another worm the crew hadn't been aware of before the apocalypse. He's thankful to have found the breaker panel behind the false wall—otherwise, they would have been vulnerable inside if any piggies came through the laboratory trapdoors.

The back of the building is wracked, with shattered glass strewn over the floor. The purchasing department lies in chaos, with dirty papers and materials stomped into the ground. Several loose papers swirl from the cross breeze, creating little tornadoes over chipped tiles. Night covers the room, with a soft moonglow cast over a cubicle with the nameplate "Brett Lowell." His jaundiced skeleton still sits in a torn black office chair, a leg jutting out to the side, one foot underneath still clinging to a brown dress shoe. The sock is slumped over, partially stuck to decaying bits of flesh. In the chair next to him sits the remains of a woman. Ben can't read her nameplate.

The stink in the air makes him dry heave, and he grips the pistol tighter. He's careful to exit the underground quietly, trying not to disturb any plants or debris that had made their way to the trapdoor that leads to Abby's lab. Scanning left and right, he sees the other trapdoors are unmolested.

Why Abby's lab?

He stands fully, looking forward at the dense woods behind the building, and that's when he sees it. The source of their strife for the past six months. The cause of the piggy invasion, the deaths of most of the employees at Soto Labs, and the infection that worked its paralysis through the hearts and lungs of another eighty percent of the population through bites, including the night elf. There it is—a blistering pustule of alien strength. Just standing there, watching him. Ben lowers his gun, his mouth folding down toward hell in sorrow.

"Oh, Abby...I'm so sorry," he groans. Her yellow, pus-blistered skin quivers as she stands firm with a wicked grin. Thick, juicy tentacles sway around her, dripping a foul, hazy substance; Ben can see they're without their black pods. *It was your spawn that has been after us. Yours that we just killed!*

The timing of her attacks still doesn't make sense to Ben. A quick thought tells him that it was this time in the middle of the night that Tyler finally transformed her after kidnapping her. His heart skips a beat. It doesn't matter anymore. He lifts the gun again with his good arm, the other remaining slack from the poison. His shooting skills have improved significantly since their encounter with Tyler at the apartment, practicing with Byron and sometimes Jerry during the day. Charles and Duane have shown no interest in shooting, preferring the safety of the worm. "I'm an old man, son!" Charles would say.

Abby's inhuman eyes scan him. Ben can't see their color, but he knows they've transformed from uncommon gray to the color of pitch. She lets out a low growl.

Ben lines up the sight. It's pointed directly at her face. Squinting through the sight, he sees her lip curl into a menacing grin, the small dimple digging into her cheek.

Click—bang!

***

Mulligan! [Return to chapter "Disturbed"] (Page 146)

CREEPS

EXTRAS

New Homeowner

A bonus short story

WHO WOULD HAVE GUESSED that when purchasing the cute 2-story foreclosure, its walls would hold many secrets? I didn't know.

The purchase occurred on a breezy spring day - the sky was crystal blue with fluffy white clouds plucked from a painting. Nothing about the flat-faced white exterior and slightly overgrown ivy wending around the front lattice suggested malice.

The interior had been refurbished. Light shafts poured through tall windows, illuminating the entire front area, highlighting tasteful light blue walls and beveled white wainscot. The selling point for me was the kitchen. Oh, the kitchen! How beautiful with white cabinets, crown molding, and quartz countertops. I was only too eager to shake hands and sign papers.

"Seventy-nine thousand? Are you sure that's all? Fully furnished and everything?"

"That's all. The home is in foreclosure, so the bank just wants something. This house isn't very popular," the agent had told me, gum-smacking between yellow-stained teeth and a crusty red lip. She smelled like cheap perfume, attempting to cover the smell of old urine.

I couldn't in good conscience pass up the deal. I had already started envisioning my stuff in the brightly lit haven.

"I'll take it," I told her with a grin. She just looked at me with a snarl.

"Is it just you? That's a lot of house for one person."

I made sure to return her grimace in kind. *Who does she think she is?*

"Yes, it's just me. But that will change in time, I hope."

She just nodded. Her thinning black curls bobbed like jellyfish as the gum continued to pop in her teeth.

"Alright, I'll meet you at the office, and we can sign the papers."

She had already turned around to crawl into her black SUV. I stood still, savoring the moment. I could easily trim the ivy and clean up the yard.

The move-in was flawless. Timely movers with nothing broken, I couldn't have asked for a more perfect service. I tipped the men well before closing myself up in the cozy interior. I had a ton of boxes but no good pieces of furniture. I was thankful that the home had come furnished, especially the living room. The room's centerpiece was an overstuffed couch dressed in old, fragrant leather. A craftsman-style coffee table came paired with it, standing atop a plush area rug that had no doubt cost a small fortune. I had never felt so lucky to stumble upon this find!

In my haste to buy the house, however, I hadn't made a thorough attempt at canvassing the upstairs, where the bedrooms were. When I originally toured the house, nothing was peculiar about the second floor. The top of the stairs joined up with the rightmost edge of the hallway. A curling wooden banister protected the first third of the hall from the floor below, with an ornate swaying chandelier dangling from the loft. My footfalls creaked on the original wood plank flooring. I remember it smelled nice up here.

Only three long strides took me to the bedroom on the left and a spare on the right. The remaining bedroom and bathroom took three more. I *did* have to use the bathroom...

I made my way to the end of the hall, turning right to grip the crystal knob. Icy fingers traced the back of my neck, prickling the little hairs there. A light feeling of unease played at my belly button. *What was that?* I flicked on the light in the bathroom.

It was only me looking back at me. I was a little sweaty and dirty, but other than that, the bathroom was clean and inviting, the fingers having retreated. *Where did that come from?* There was a faint scent of cinnamon and vanilla in the air. I looked down to see that the previous owner had left an open candle sitting on the counter. Its smell permeated the room, creating a pleasant atmosphere I could not deny. A crystal vase full of fake white daisies stood sentinel on the counter, paired well with the ivory shower curtain and light green walls.

Well, I had come in here to do my business, and I planned to do that. Another fortunate thing - there was a fresh roll of toilet paper. *What a find!*

After completing my ritual, I stood at the mirror, taking in the cinnamon vanilla fragrance - a warmth I knew would be gone the second I stepped through the door. Sure enough, the hallway brought a cold heat that burrowed through the skin of my brow, releasing clammy sweat and an anxiety that I felt in my bladder. *Surely you must not have to pee again?* I just needed to reach the bedroom, that's all—three long strides.

The bedroom was beautiful. All of the walls except for one had been painted in such a lovely shade of beige, with the remaining wall a striking deep burgundy. The instant I entered that room, I was at peace. The cold sweat evaporated, and I was no longer plagued by anxiety. *A great place to call your bedroom!*

The agent hadn't lied when she said it was fully furnished. This room had an amazing cherry wood four-poster! The mattress was clean, with no bedding. I snapped my fingers in defeat but could only smile at how great this whole experience had been. I had sheets and a comforter, no problem. The movers had kindly stacked all bedroom boxes in the correct room. They stood in the corner, waiting for unpacking.

First things first, I had to try out the mattress. I plopped on top, sinking about three inches. This mattress was like new - almost as if the previous owner had bought it and chose to sleep on the floor the whole time, leaving it in pristine condition. Looking back at the bedroom door, a curiosity gnawed at me. Something drew me back to those cold, loveless fingers at the end of the hall.

An odd door, about half the size of a regular door, had been there the whole time, right next to the bathroom. The handle was nondescript, with a slight indentation in the wall, as if intentionally hiding. I had only happened to glimpse it from the flickering bulb in the hall playing at its shadow. A linen closet, perhaps?

I stared at it, hesitant. *Why though? This house was amazing.* My finger traced the rim of the hidden handle. It was the type you rolled your fingers underneath and pulled outward. The door did not need convincing to open. Once the handle clicked, the door slowly swung open without assistance and bumped to a stop against the opposite wall.

It was a small room. Fully furnished. It looked well-kept but old. There was a single couch pushed against a sloping, butter-yellow wall. The couch had an old style— brown, orange, plaid, and soft-looking. A small table sat next to it, the color of honey oak. Atop the table was perched what appeared to be a decades-old ham radio.

The icy fingers had returned, raking their blue coldness up the back of my neck and into my thick hair. I had frozen on the spot, looking into that room and not knowing why. Something about it ached in my gut. The ghostly hand at the back of my head gently urged me forward. *Just check it out... it's a whole other room!*

Come inside. The radio crackled, barely audible. Was that in my head?

I had to crouch to get inside. Once past the small door, I could stand fully but barely. *Why hadn't the agent told me to look here?* She had to have known there was a room. It smelled like dust—old dust, but oddly not unpleasant either. There was a heaviness to the room, almost nostalgic and comforting but terrifying. My skin prickled, and the silence deafened me. I felt like I was floating in a wad of cotton. *What is this room?*

My legs had turned to stone. I had to use every ounce of my willpower to fight the thickness of the room. Stiff-legged, I tromped to the door, crouched, and entered the hallway. I closed the door, took three strides, and felt calm again. My legs became fleshy and mobile, and I could feel the air drifting over my skin. *How neat is this house?*

I needed some air—trimming the ivy sounded like a good idea at the time, so I set out to do just that. Armed with a small set of garden clippers and a white, sweat-stained bandanna fixed over my brow, I skipped down the porch steps to survey the front of the house.

As I studied the exterior, I realized this was a room built into one of the house's eaves. It made some sense, but not complete sense. Surveying the outside of the house, this room was too big to fit in that eave. Even though the room was indeed small, it was still too big. *Okay, you got your air. Go back inside and investigate.* Leaving the ivy untrimmed, I couldn't pull myself from the allure of that couch and ham radio.

I again found myself at the end of the hall, cold fingers dancing through my hair. My stomach squeezed and ached with alarm bells and curiosity. The door swung open. My eyes were fixed on that radio.

Welcome back. The static crackled, the voice clear. *Wait, what is that?*

Another door the height of the last but half the width stood next to the radio. *Is this finally the linen closet?*

I open the new door.

The micro room couldn't even be called a room. It was a yawning black maw— a deep cockpit of fear and longing. Waves of unease coursed from its depths, rippling through every fiber of my torso and freezing my legs into place like marble columns supporting a fried egg over easy. Curiosity split my mind, and I couldn't tear my eyes away from the undulating blackness.

The wall pulled me against it with an invisible tug. I couldn't move even if I tried. Did I even *want* to try? My skin stuck to the plaster, gluing itself in place. I felt like clay hardening slowly in the sun, melding with the plaster. The skin of my forearms crackled and spit tiny plumes of dust.

I felt my legs collapse under my jeans, the fabric dangling life-lessly from the sloped wall, connected only by my damp torso. My favorite shoes, the black and plaid custom chucks, clattered to the floor. I knew then why the agent hadn't shown this room.

The back of my head flattened against the vault of the wall. Crushing noises filled my ears as my brain began to dry up, and my skull formed parched salt cracks. My eyeballs hazed over, blurring the subtle definitions of the couch fibers until it became a swirling blob of orange and brown. I could no longer see with human eyes. I could only feel.

The air tickled the tip of my nose. Soon, it would no longer be the tip. My face stretched and widened over the old plaster. My clothing fell to a heap on the floor. My skin was butter yellow. I could feel it. *What a great find this house had been. I was so lucky to find it.*

***

The clear blue sky showcases fluffy white clouds drifting with the light breeze. A sharp couple with their two young children stand outside on the walkway of a charming white 2-story.

"That's all they're asking? For real? And you said fully furnished, too, right?" the man asks, stroking the older daughter's smooth ponytail.

"Yeah, that's right. It's in foreclosure, so the bank wants to get some money out of it..." The agent smacks gum under a painted red lip. She grins.

ABOUT THE AUTHOR

R.E. Holding grew up in the Midwest in the 80s and 90s, often finding herself on the dirty low-pile carpets of Waldenbooks reading the newest Christopher Pike YA horror. She's an avid lover of stories of all kinds, whether it be through books, movies, tabletop games, etc., with a particular penchant for the things that go bump in the night.

A scientist by day, she writes horror, sci-fi, and fantasy at night. If not writing, reading, watching movies, or tending to family, she's making soap on YouTube. Follow the links below to visit CCB or LH Soaps!

www.cliffcavebooks.com
www.lhsoaps.com

Acknowledgments

Writing a book is hard. Anyone who tells you otherwise is fooling you, or they are Stephen King. I won't put words in his mouth, but I would imagine he'd say it's not that bad.

Anyway, Metaxysm is my first full novel (and it's still short!) that started as my National Novel Writer's Month pet project in 2021 that I didn't imagine would go anywhere. I've participated in NaNoWriMo since 2008, "won" a few years, but only used it as an exercise in writing discipline. Why is Metaxysm different? I don't know, to be honest. After finishing NaNo in 2021, I turned my back on Metaxysm and carried on with my life.

I had a job as a project manager and found myself in my down-time talking to the engineers about my book and how cool I thought it was with the different endings and all that stuff. The more I talked about it, the more I thought about the world of Abby, Ben, and Byron. Tyler didn't originally have any complexity – he was a straight douche. Well, I lost that job and had all the time in the world to flesh out the book, so I did. Tyler became more nuanced, Ben got a better backstory, and Byron, well... he's my favorite.

I'm so thankful for my ever-patient husband, who supported my jobless self at the time while I beat through this novel one draft at a time, even if he had no desire to read it. Losing that job was really the kick in the pants I needed to finish this book— and as an additional bonus, I actually started to write my first fantasy series based on a world I started building back in 2003 (and a nightmare I had in college). I had Worldbuilder's sickness... now, I'm excited to say that I've started actually writing that monster, and book 1 is available now, with the prologue in the back of this book.

There are several people I can't thank enough for supporting my efforts along the way. The first person I'll shout out is Paul Adam, the fantastic artist behind the cover illustration. I started as a fan of his work back in the late 90s/early 00s, and while I've never personally met him, he's always entertained my dumb questions and intrusions into his world. I'm so excited to have finally collaborated with him on something. I'd also like to thank my niece, Cailey "porcelain princess" George, for going through this manuscript and fixing dumb errors! Angela Brown, for being a supportive copy-editing professional, and last but not least, Delphya Tillman for just being my hype-(wo)man! Your encouragement has always been so uplifting, and I hope I've been able to do the same for you!

Reaper's Gamble, Book 1 Sample

PROLOGUE

Waves of desert heat pulsed over Loren's skin, but all he felt was cold. He strained to sense his surroundings, seeing wave after wave of yellow dust blowing over the dunes. A grinding static muffled his eardrums, drowning out the screams of his friend.

None of his books had ever taught him this. No book ever told him what it was like to die.

Scan the code to get the ebook directly from Cliff Cave Books!

Scan this code to get the ebook and print copies wherever available!

VISIT THE SUBSTACK AT

www.reholdingauthor.com

FEATURES OF THE SITE:
- Updates & Reviews
- Upcoming Works
- Soap Making
- Special Requests

Join the newsletter to receive CCB updates, special offers, reviews, giveaways, and more. Stay in touch!

ALSO BY R.E. HOLDING

Not all vampires are created equal...
Filled with dark humor and suspense, Hillbilly Vamp takes readers on a wild roller coaster ride through the twisted minds of backwoods creatures who possess an insatiable hunger that must be met at any cost.
If you like dark humor or horror comedies and the supernatural, you'll love the antics in Hillbilly Vamp!

"Who knew being an adult had to be so violent..."
Introducing a colorful world where jobs aren't so ordinary, perks come with a price, and secrets are governed by Audun, the capital of the world.
For fans of slow-burn fantasy, twists, hidden identities, and fated relationships. Reaper's Gamble is book 1 in the series.

LET'S CONNECT!

If you would like to see more from Cliff Cave Books, visit the link HERE, or scan/tap the QR code below:

R.E. Holding, also has a LinkTree. If you're interested in more works by her, visit the link HERE, or scan/tap the QR code below:

Scan me